I0546047

What's her Secret?

COVERT AFFAIR

GERALDINE O'HARA

COVERT AFFAIR

Chapter One

I stood outside The Rusty Nail, feeling guilty that I was still keeping a secret from my friends. I'd kept one before, from Leon—the man I'd fancied the pants off for ages—but that was out in the open between us now. This new secret was mine *and* his, and we'd agreed to set things in motion tonight so it wouldn't be something to hide for much longer. I'd have to lie—again—in order to pull this off, but what was one more on top of all the others I'd told?

I took a deep breath and put my hand on one of the doors. It was cold even through my gloves, and if I didn't get inside soon I'd freeze my tits off. The weather had changed drastically over the past week, going from reasonable autumn to harsh and evil winter. Of course, it had taken me ages to find my gloves and scarf tonight, but I was glad of the time it had taken. I'd needed the extra minutes to steel myself.

You can still keep this secret for a while longer.

I pushed the door and went inside.

The pub was packed—unusual for a Thursday night but there were a load of beefy men propping up the bar, some rugby team or other gathering after their match. It gave the pub a claustrophobic air, one I wasn't used to and didn't like. I preferred it the way it usually was, where we could stand without anyone in our personal space.

I stared around for my friends. Wedged between a man with biceps bigger than my thighs and another whose tattoos obliterated most of his skin, Jen and the blokes in our little gang looked more than put out. I smiled. We were used to having the place pretty much to ourselves, and with the pub being our local, outsiders were seen as interlopers. Tom cats spraying on another's patch.

I'd been keeping a secret from them for a while now. Well, from Jen and Marshall. Gary knew about my relationship with Leon—him being his best friend and the one to finally get us together—but me and Leon had been sneaking around for a few months now. I'd had the mad idea that us being together and our group knowing about it might have upset the balance. We'd gotten along so well up until now that revealing something different had me cautious. Why rock the boat? Why spoil what was working?

Because if we didn't, we'd have to sneak around forever and I couldn't stand the thought of that. Mind you, we'd shared news of our loves and relationships in the past, had talked about the men or women we'd been seeing, so me being with Leon wasn't much different, was it?

Keeping the secret had wreaked havoc on my nerves, especially the past couple of weeks. Jen had seemed suspicious as to why I wasn't going out with her as much—trips to the shops for new clothes or makeup, stuff like that—and had even asked if she'd done something wrong. I'd assured her she hadn't but I don't think she bought it.

Besides, the irritation of not being able to reach out and touch Leon in any way other than in friendship grated on my nerves too. The man was on my mind twenty-four-seven, so to pretend he wasn't had become a bit of a bind. At times I'd had to stop myself planting a kiss on his cheek or holding his hand while we drank ourselves silly with our gang. He'd slipped up once or twice too, putting his hand on the bottom of my back or absent-mindedly rubbing my thigh if we were sitting at one of the tables.

Things had to change. Whether the others liked it or not.

I pushed through a group of rugby players, assaulted by the overpowering smell of deodorant and aftershave where they'd obviously had a post-game shower. The mix was cloying, and I'd swear they pressed around me, trying to block me in. One of them pinched my bum, and I turned in a tight circle, studying all their faces to determine which one held a guilty look.

"Who did that?" I asked, frowning. "Don't you know it's rude to do that?"

"Rude's our game," one of them said, a short fella with cauliflower ears that would look right at home on a plate of Sunday roast.

"Well, whatever your game is, I'm not playing. Could you move, please? I'd like to get past."

"We could," Cauli Ears said, "but I don't think we will. You fit more than nicely there. What's it like being surrounded by a load of sexy blokes?"

Sexy? They were average as far as I was concerned, but judging by their expressions they all felt the same as Cauli. God's gift and all that. I found their attitude boring. How many years had I gone out with men just like them, thinking they were the kind of men I deserved—or, to be honest, the only kind of man available?

Too many to count.

"I wouldn't know what it's like," I said. "Because I've never been surrounded by them."

Cauli narrowed his eyes. I'd hit a nerve. He reminded me of a man I'd slept with just before I'd started seeing Leon. The type who thought he was the best-looking man on the planet and that I should have been grateful he'd chosen me to fuck. At the time I'd been exceptionally pleased he had—stupid cow—but since then I'd learnt that people like him were in abundance and long-lasting relationships weren't something they seemed to want. This Cauli was no different, I suspected.

"That was a bit bitchy," Cauli said.

They pressed closer to me, so much so my arms were trapped by my sides. I glanced over at my friends, trying to catch their attention, but they hadn't seen me come in and were deep in conversation.

Fuck it.

"It was," I said. "And me screaming would be even bitchier because then you'd most probably get kicked out. So if you want to finish your pints…"

No way was I going to be cowed by the likes of Cauli and his cohorts. Those days were well and truly bloody gone. It helped that I was a regular here and that any shout from me would have several people running to sort them out.

Thankfully, they got the message and stepped back—but only enough so that I could squeeze out of their circle into another throng. How many men were on a sodding rugby team anyway? Or were their fans in here as well?

Annoyed and relieved at the same time, I pressed on and made it to my friends. I stood by Leon—probably more for comfort than anything else—and pulled a face to show them I wasn't best pleased.

"What's up?" Jen asked.

She lived in a flat next to mine above the Chinese restaurant down the road. Since the night I'd first fucked Leon, she'd been seeing Gary—and she thought I didn't know. I'd often pondered on the fact that we were both keeping secrets from one another— something we'd vowed never to do—but had let it go. Maybe it was time we grew up and moved on from the high-school mentality of always telling one another the ins and outs of the cat's arsehole with regards to our lives. I didn't find the prospect alarming but had a feeling Jen would find it difficult to mind her own business. I loved her, I really did, but she was a nosey mare.

"Them lot," I said, jerking my head to the side to indicate the arseholes behind us.

"Oh, I *know*." She stared at them over my shoulder, giving her best no-nonsense glare. Men had been reduced to withering wrecks by it in the past. "Rolled in half an hour ago as though they own the bloody place. Loud bastards, too."

"Pissing me right off," Leon said.

I looked at him to determine how pissed off he was—and realized he'd possibly caught part of the rugby players encasing me. If they'd given me any real trouble he'd have stepped in. If we were going to keep our relationship secret, he had to act as he would if we were only friends, and that meant intervening only when a friend should.

"Me too," I said. "Anyway, I've got something to tell you all."

Leon turned away to lift his pint from the bar and take a sip. We'd discussed this before we'd met up tonight. I was to make my announcement then he'd casually make his.

"What's that?" Jen widened her eyes, her face alight with interest.

"I'm going away for a week," I said. "By myself."

"What?" she shrieked. "Who the hell goes away on their own?"

"I do." I smiled. "I thought I'd take some time out. You know, get to know who I am."

"Discover your hidden self," Marshall said. "Going all zen on us, are you?"

I laughed. "No, nothing like that. I just want..." I couldn't think what to say. Me going away was like a nun gleefully diving headlong into an orgy—it just didn't happen.

"Going away myself," Leon said, saving me. "Work."

"Since when did you go away for work?" Gary asked, winking.

"Since yesterday." Leon took a gulp of beer.

Shit, are they going to rat us out?

"Boss usually sends some other bloke but he's off sick." Leon sniffed casually. "So I said I'd go. It's only to Blackpool."

"Oh, for God's sake!" I said, hoping the response of surprise I'd practiced earlier hadn't come off as fake. "*I'm* going there!"

"Well I'm buggered," Leon said. "They say real life's stranger than fiction."

I couldn't look at him. I had a feeling we'd been too transparent. Instead, I stared at the others in turn.

From what I could see, none of them seemed to have caught on to our subterfuge.

"We could meet up if you like," I said, busying myself by fumbling in my bag for my purse. I needed a stiff drink—a large one. "But if not, no worries."

"Nope, that'll be fine," he said. "May as well. I won't have much to do in the evenings. Hadn't liked the thought of spending it watching TV in the hotel."

"But they have *porn* channels, mate," Gary said. "You could watch a whole series of them. Whack-off heaven."

Jen gave him one of her cutting glares. I stifled a laugh and smiled at Leon.

When we got back the plan was to make out that we'd suddenly found we wanted to be together. Telling them we'd had a wild week in Blackpool that had surprised the hell out of us was better than saying we'd been carrying on behind their backs for months. Not that it was any of their business that we had, but belonging to a group of friends who usually shared most things meant I'd felt a fraud and a horrible person for keeping it from them.

"So that's the zen angle out for you, Mandy," Marshall said, grinning. "You know, being by yourself and all that."

"It is." I pushed between him and Gary. "'Scuse me a sec, I need a drink."

I propped my elbows on the bar and caught the server's attention. I ordered my usual vodka—a double, though—and that first sip was heaven. My mouth had gone dry with lies, but now it was sufficiently wet I turned to face the group again. Leon gave me one of his secret looks – '*I need to speak to you for a minute…*' – and I let out a dramatic sigh.

"Why does that *always* happen when I get in here?" I said. "I need the bloody loo again." I put my glass on the bar. "Watch that for me will you, Jen?"

Without waiting for a response, I wandered through the crowd toward the toilets. I had to go past Cauli and his friends so kept my gaze ahead and my chin high. As the bodies thinned out a bit, I breathed easier and took a left down the corridor that led to the ladies. About halfway down I heard soft footfalls on the carpet and smiled. Leon had gotten away quicker than he usually did. Once at the end of the corridor I turned to face the entrance—to find Cauli right in front of me, his width filling the space along with his cheap-smelling cologne. My heart skittered a bit, but I was well used to dealing with men like him.

"Um, excuse me?" I said, sidestepping to make it clear I wanted to get away.

"Why, have you had a lapse in the arse department?" He smiled, one of those smarmy efforts that told the world he found himself most amusing.

"And you think a woman's going to find you attractive when you say things like that?" I shook my head. "No wonder you're single."

"Married, actually."

"Poor her then," I said, glancing down at his hand to see no wedding ring or evidence that he'd ever worn one.

His expression changed from smug self-appreciation to something sinister. My stomach muscles tensed and I had the urge to shove at his chest so he went sprawling.

"You *are* one of those bitchy types, aren't you." He stepped forward.

His chest was inches from mine. One of his shoes nudged my boot. He didn't scare me—probably because I knew Leon was on his way — but in another situation he might have. What gave him the right to do this, to follow me then menace me in a corridor? Anger ignited, and I lifted my knee, connecting it with his groin. He crumpled a bit but not as much as I'd hoped. Moving closer, controlling his grimace, he pressed me against the wall. I did what I'd wanted to earlier and pushed at his chest, but he wasn't going anywhere. All muscle, he stood his ground.

"Married I might be," he said, beer breath in my face, "but at least she isn't a cow like you."

"Which makes me wonder why you're even bothering with me. If she's so wonderful, why the need to pick up other women? Fuck off out of my way." That kind of line had worked in the past — being a loud-mouthed ladette had had its advantages.

He moved — quickly — going backwards with such speed it took me by surprise. Until I saw he'd been dragged away from me by Leon then carted to the other end of the corridor. Leon said something to him, right in his ear, but I couldn't make out what it was. Going by Cauli's face, it wasn't anything pleasant. A surge of pride went through me, and I wanted to whisper 'My hero!' and flutter my hand at my chest like some long-ago film star.

I refrained.

Instead, heart going crazy, I swallowed and watched. Leon shoved Cauli, who disappeared from view, then turned to stare at me down the corridor. I could have just run to him, thrown myself into his arms for saving me, kissed him madly then told him I was his for the taking. His masterly behavior had got me going, but having it away in The Rusty Nail wasn't an option. Not one I'd contemplated before anyway.

There's a first time for everything…

Leon stalked toward me, his face full of thunder, his fists bunched. I went weak at the knees and flattened my palms to the wall, my breathing unsteady. Fuck, he was gorgeous. He reached me, pushed his body into mine and gripped my wrists. Holding them up over my head and to the wall, he kissed me hard, taking away my ability to think of anything else but him. I kissed him back then reality kicked in. We were in The Rusty Nail. We could get caught. I snatched my mouth from his.

"Stop it," I said. "We could be spotted and I—"

"I don't care anymore."

He stared at me with such intensity in his gaze it had me realizing all over again why I loved him, why he turned me on like he did, why he was the man I wanted to be with. If I were bolder I'd let him fuck me right where I stood.

He broke our connection. Glanced to the door on his right. Gestured to it with his head. "You up for it?"

I looked at the door. It had a sign on the front. *Staff Only.*

"What's in there?" I asked.

"No idea." He opened it.

A clatter of tinny thuds filtered out. I couldn't see where it led but Leon smiled.

"Sounds like the cellar's down there," he said, letting the door go. "Like I said, you up for it?"

Was I? Could I have a bit of one-on-one time with him beside the beer barrels and their hissing mechanisms knowing someone might come down at any time?

Yes, I could. I was Mad Mandy, after all, the woman who was seen as crazy, wild and up for anything.

Chapter Two

Leon pulled the door open again and slipped through the gap first. Normally, he'd have opened it for me then followed, but I supposed he had my welfare in mind. We didn't know if a member of staff was down there, and I was thankful he'd taken the lead. If we encountered anyone, I'd leave it up to him to offer an explanation.

I couldn't see much. There was a faint light but it didn't reach where we were.

"There are some stairs here," Leon said. "Be careful."

I held onto his shoulders as he went down, my tummy a riot of madness in my apprehensive yet excited state. What we were doing was so damn risky. Part of me worried about that but another part didn't give a shit. I felt wild and naughty, free somehow, to be doing something like this.

It wasn't every day you got the chance to fuck in a pub cellar.

We reached the bottom and I looped my arm into the crook of Leon's. The cellar was cold and dank, smelling of beer, damp and some kind of cleaner I assumed they used to wash the pipes. In the meager light I made out rows of metal barrels lining one wall, said pipes going up through the ceiling. The walls were bare brick that looked rough to the touch. All in all, it was a grim location.

Did I really want to have sex in here?

You know you do. Go on. Do it.

Something hissed then clicked, and I darted closer to Leon.

"It's only someone pouring a lager upstairs," he whispered.

"What if someone's down here?"

"They're not. Only the barmaid and that Northern fella's working tonight and they were both behind the bar when I came to find you."

He took my hand and led me across an uneven cement floor to a dark corner. There, a wine rack had been bolted to the wall. I let my gaze roam in search of spiders but saw none. Then again I wouldn't. It was murky and creepy. Maybe the ugly eight-legged buggers were hiding in the shadows. Wherever they were they could stay there. I didn't fancy *that* kind of tickle in my knickers, thank you.

"Come here, woman," Leon said, pressing me to the wall and sliding his hand beneath my skirt.

I let out a giggle of surprise.

"You've got the smoothest legs. Fucking sexy."

I shivered. His words when we got together like this always sounded so raw, him the bit of rough I craved. Yet he was gentle at the same time, careful never to go too far. At times I *wanted* him to go further, to push the boundaries and take me whatever way he wanted—hard, fast, without mercy. Was he like me, still trying to be his real self? To find out who he was? I decided to test that, see where it went.

"Fuck me," I said, butterflies dancing in my belly at my boldness. "Fuck me hard. Give it to me as though you haven't had sex for weeks. Like you can't get enough."

"I never can get enough, not of you."

He dipped his head to kiss my neck, sending more shivers sprawling over my body. His hot breath coasted across my skin, ribbons of desire streaking into my cunt. I groaned, wanting him to rip my clothes off and take me like an animal. Too polite, he wouldn't—unless I goaded him on.

"Go on," I said. "Get your hands inside my knickers. Finger my cunt."

I heard him swallow and he paused in kissing my neck.

"Jesus Christ," he whispered. "The things you do to me."

"Tell me what."

"The way you've got a dirty mouth on you. The way you turn into a woman who knows what she wants and isn't afraid to say so. The way you"—he panted, moaned—"get my dick so damn hard."

"And is it hard?" I reached down to check, stroking the hardness then fumbling to get his jeans open. "Yes, it's hard. Hard enough to shove it in me and ride me ragged." I was on a roll, in the mood to get him going to the point where he couldn't hold back if he tried. "And you want to ride me, don't you. Get in my warm pussy and ram in and out."

He didn't answer with words—instead he yanked at my knickers in an effort to pull them down. He let them drop to my ankles, and I stepped out of them, leaving them on the floor. At that moment I didn't care if I never saw them again and the landlord found them in the morning.

"God, the fucking feel of you," he said.

He rucked up my skirt then slid his hand between my legs, pushing his fingers into my wet folds and mimicking what he'd do with his cock. In and out, in and out. I parted my legs farther and raised my hips, hoping to catch my clit on the heel of his hand. He kissed my neck again, his breathing heavy and warm.

"That's it," I said. "Finger-fuck me just like that."

I was soaked, my cunt more than ready to take whatever he wanted to give. He plunged his fingers in, stroking my clit with his thumb. I jolted, his touch electric, and shuddered at the fizzle of sensation that spread from there throughout my slit.

"God, that's so good," I said.

He stopped me talking with a kiss that curled my toes and set my cunt on fire. I keened, canting my hips higher, shoving myself into him, wanting him to make me come so hard I screamed. I undid his jeans, took his cock out then wanked him, loving the weighty feel of him in my hand. His cock was smooth, the skin so soft, yet his erection was solid and something I wanted more of—in my cunt, mouth, arse, I didn't care. Wherever would suit me fine. I circled my thumb over his cock tip as he circled his over my clit. I moaned into his mouth in a frantic bid to kiss him so hard he'd know how much he meant to me.

He broke the kiss to lick my neck then nuzzle my earlobe. He bit lightly, and the pleasure-pain from that fled right down to between my legs. I clenched my pussy, wanting to hold off the orgasm that pushed to be set free. I didn't want to come until he was inside me, seated right to the damn hilt and filling me completely.

"I need your cock," I panted out, massaging it faster. "Quickly." I opened my legs wider, jerking my wet cunt at his cock. "Feel that? Feel how wet I am?"

"You're a filthy little—"

I silenced him with a kiss, and he settled his cock at my entrance. I waited, waited for him to surge in and set me free. He paused, teasing, knowing how much I'd want him to get inside me now—now, damn it.

He pushed up and in, his width stretching me, his balls meeting with the bottom curves of my arse. I moved my mouth from his to bite down on his shoulder as he hefted me upwards. My arse scraped the rough wall and I wrapped my legs around his waist, crossing them at the ankles. Holding me confined in the small space, he withdrew then surged back in, repeating the motion, speeding up with every thrust.

"There you go," I said breathlessly. "There you fucking well go. That's it, you know exactly what I want and how I want it."

His lower abdomen rubbed my clit, his gyrations ensuring we didn't lose that skin-on-skin contact. He changed his thrusts to shallower ones, going in deeper, his pelvis pressing harder. Pleasure built, and the thought that someone could come down for a bottle of wine or to change a barrel had it skyrocketing. I gripped his arse, digging my nails into his flesh. He kissed my collarbone, tugging my top down, the back of the neck scraping my skin. The material creaked, gave way a bit, and he wrenched open a couple of buttons, exposing my chest. He freed a breast from my bra, dipping his head and sucking on my nipple. It peaked in his mouth, and he swirled his tongue around it then lightly bit down.

"Ah, ah, ah," I said, loving what he was doing.

He bit again, with extra pressure this time, then drew his head back to elongate my nipple. I arched my back as best I could, wanting him to pull again, to give me that pinch of pleasure in my tit that always had me groaning. He read me well, doing as I'd silently asked, and I raised one hand to clutch the back of his head. His hair between my fingers, I clenched my hand into a fist and eased his head back until my breast lifted and the pleasure-pain increased tenfold. This was what it was all about, him and me like this, primal sex that had me wanting more, more, more.

"Yeah, you know how to suck," I gasped out. "You know how I love it. And you know how to fuck."

He grunted, bit again, and my cunt spasmed. His cock felt bigger then, as though it had expanded. He throbbed inside me, and my clit pulsed along with it. I scored my nails down his arse, pulled him closer, as close as he could get. He let my nipple go, and for a wonderful, delicious few seconds I basked in the numbness there, then the cold air as it peaked my nipple further. He splayed his fingers on my lower belly, using his thumb to stimulate my clit. Strong, circular movements and I was undone.

Bliss radiated, spreading from my cunt to the rest of my body. I tipped my head back, grazing it on the wall, my hair catching on the uneven surface, my neck exposed for him to kiss, lick, nip and suck.

"Oh, God, you sexy fuck," I breathed. "You sexy fucking fuck."

"Christ, keep talking while I"—he gave a particularly sharp thrust—"get you off."

"You're getting me off. Getting"—I gritted my teeth to brace myself for the onslaught I knew was coming—"me off."

There it was, that burst of pleasure, careening so fast I almost couldn't take it all in. I closed my eyes and drowned in it, crying out and clutching his hair harder, his arse harder. His dick throbbed again, a set of beats that matched my rapid pulse, then he tweaked my nipple between finger and thumb, kissing me with so much need that I felt it.

He came, shuddering, stilling as spunk came out of him. He pistoned in and out again, stuttered words that I couldn't understand leaving him and me. I moaned, stifling the sound against his shoulder, letting the sensations ebb and flow, take me wherever they would. Heat warmed my skin, sweat beading at my temples, and I loved every damn aftershock that juddered through me.

"I love you," he said, giving one last thrust-shunt.

"And I fucking love you."

He stopped all movement to look at me in the darkness. I made out the shape of him, the slight glint of his eyes created by the light coming from a dim bulb behind an opaque glass shade a few meters away. He was out of breath, shaking slightly, and lowered me to the floor. I stood on wobbly legs, staring up at him, and cupped his face in one hand. His stubble rasped my palm and his cheek bunched — a smile, I guessed.

"We're so good together, you and me," he said.

"So bloody good."

He popped my bra back, covering my tit, then did my top up. I watched him in wonder, still, even after a few months, unable to believe he was mine. That this wasn't just some affair that would die out when he got bored of me. We were too in tune for that, too close, and our sex life was off the charts. It could have been the secrecy of it all, but I didn't think so. Some people just gelled.

"We should go back up," I said.

"We should but it doesn't mean I want to. I could stay down in this stinky cellar with you all night." He stroked my cheek.

I held his hand to keep it still and gazed at him, not seeing anything much but knowing exactly what was there. I knew how his eyebrows were shaped, like gently curving rainbows. I knew that if he were smiling he'd have dimples. And I knew his eyes held sincerity and that I'd see it if only the light were brighter. But the darkness meant nothing—I saw it all anyway.

I let his hand go then bent to pick up my knickers. Now our encounter was over, I *did* mind if the landlord found them. I didn't bother to put them back on, though, slipping them in my pocket instead. I pulled my skirt down, smoothing it and not caring if wrinkles had formed where it had been bunched up. If anyone saw it and suspected what we'd been doing— it no longer mattered. Yes, we'd prefer to reveal our secret when we got home from our holiday, but, why the hell had we *really* hidden it for so long? Why had we snuck around? All because we didn't want to hurt our friends' feelings?

"I want to spend the rest of my life with you, you know that, right?" I said.

"I know it. Same goes for me. Every day. I can't imagine not seeing you every day."

"How did we manage before? Without each other?"

"Badly." He chuckled. "I drifted from one bird to the next, all the time wishing they were you. And they weren't, never could be. No one could match up to you, Mandy."

God, he said the nicest things.

I didn't trust myself to speak so took his hand and led him toward the stairs. I saw now that they were rickety, old and wooden, something I'd missed on our way down. I'd been too excited to give much of a shit.

"Will we do the usual?" I asked. "You going back first then me following?"

"No, not this time. Not with that arsehole up there — if he's still there."

I thought of the rugby player and how he'd made me feel. I didn't want to be alone in that corridor again. "I'll go back first, shall I?"

Leon started up the stairs. "D'you know what? Fuck it. We'll both go back together. I doubt they've even noticed how long we've been gone."

I wished we didn't have to join them. My time with Leon was still private, something to keep to myself, a treasure no one else knew about.

And he was a treasure. My very own diamond, and once tomorrow came he'd be able to sparkle like never before. I couldn't wait to get away and be with him twenty-four-seven. For now, though, we had to get through the evening like we had so many times before, apart, only looking at each other as friends, keeping up the pretense that's all we were.

I followed him down the corridor then out into the main part of the pub. We wove through the crowd, and I was pleased to see that the hateful rugby man had gone, as had his friends. Before Jen could give me the third degree, I gulped back some of my now warm vodka — the ice had melted — then launched into a conversation with her about some woman who had jumped the queue in the post office at lunchtime. She rolled her eyes at the appropriate moments, but I caught her looking at Gary more than once. I smiled, knowing how she felt, and spent the rest of the evening avoiding Leon's gaze, talking so much crap I thought everyone would be able to smell it.

The things we do for love…

Chapter Three

This secrecy business was a killer.

Jen stood on the landing outside our flats. She'd caught me as I was leaving to meet Leon. I'd been so quiet, too, padding around my bedroom, then making sure I didn't nudge any of my cups on my mug tree in the kitchen so they tapped against the adjoining wall. Those walls were thin, though, and if she hadn't been drunk as a skunk on the night I'd first fucked Leon, she'd have heard every moan and groan.

I wondered what she was doing up so early. I hadn't heard her moving around next door either. Had she mooched about the same as me, not wanting me to know she was up? She didn't usually leave until after ten. Had she been waiting out here on purpose, ready to catch me before I left? Last night I hadn't given her a chance to probe, to ask the many questions she normally bombarded me with. I knew the fact that I had originally planned to go away alone — as far as she was concerned, anyway — would be bugging her. She needed to learn to mind her own business at times, to know when to back off, but it seemed that when it came to me she didn't know how to do that.

She was bundled up in a red woolen coat and long black scarf. Looking less than ready to go to work, she appeared tired and hungover, and that wasn't surprising. She'd had quite a few vodkas in The Rusty Nail and the more she'd drunk, the more open she'd been in touching Gary. If she were trying to keep their relationship secret she wasn't doing a very good job of it. She blinked, yawned, and I felt sorry for her having to work all day. Still, she only had a few hours to get through and she could begin her weekend.

Shagging Gary through it all, I suspected.

"Morning!" She sounded bright enough.

"Hi, Jen." I held back a sigh. I just wanted to be away, on my travels.

"How are you getting to Blackpool, bus or train?" she asked, twirling a length of her hair around a finger.

That was her usual gesture when she was after something, be it a favor or information. I braced myself for an onslaught of questions I didn't want to answer and stared at her circling finger. Her nails had been done recently, at Glorious Talons I'd bet, where the lovely Vietnamese woman always called everyone *dahleen* and offered cups of tea or coffee for customers to sip while she glued on acrylic tips. Or, if she had her way, zebra stripes or 'Somethin' glittery, you like, my dahleen?' I hadn't accompanied Jen when she'd asked me to go with her—too interested in seeing Leon—and had gone by myself one lunchtime last week. And no, I hadn't opted for zebra-striped or glittery nails. Plain white did me nicely.

"Train," I said. It was a lie, of course it was, and one of many I'd told her recently.

"Quite a long way, Blackpool," she said, staring down at my canvas suitcase on wheels.

It was more like one of those shopping trolleys old grannies used except mine wasn't tartan and didn't smell of potatoes or carrots where the market man had poured vegetables directly into it. They were trendy now anyway, and mine being baby pink with white spots was so cute. It even had a matching toiletries bag, something I hadn't been able to get over when I'd bought it. I'd almost let out a little wee at the time.

It was the simple things…

"Yes, but I always liked going there as a kid so thought I'd go again." I locked my front door. "The theme park has changed so much, I hear. And, you know, I could do with reliving some memories. Put some past to bed. Come back refreshed and whatnot."

"I'm surprised you didn't ask me to go with you. A bit hurt, actually. We always do everything together, you know that." She pouted.

I paused in putting my keys into my handbag. They slipped from my fingers and hit something inside. That sound, it made me think of finality, the thud of The End. In a way it was. The end of my friendship with Jen in that we'd gone everywhere as a pair and shared it all. Things wouldn't be the same for us when I got back, but wasn't that the way life went? People moved on, and just because I'd be announcing my so-called new relationship status with Leon, it didn't mean things had to change that drastically. Although they already had. I hadn't been hanging out with her as much, meeting Leon over her, but then again, she'd been meeting Gary, albeit without me supposedly knowing, so we were even on the 'Abandon Our Friendship' score.

"I wanted..." How would I put this without letting the cat out of the bag? "I just need some time out, okay?" I winced, hating the way impatience had seeped into my tone.

"Hardly time out if you're meeting up with Leon while you're there."

She wasn't about to let this go, and I sensed she'd be snippy if we continued the conversation. Jen in a strop wasn't something I wanted today. It was supposed to be happy, no hassles, exciting. Jen had unfortunately soured that—or had that been me allowing her to do it? I'd read somewhere, probably online in one of those random posts on Facebook, that only you can allow someone to make you feel like shit. I agreed with it to a point, but when that someone went all out to piss you off, saying things that took the shine off your good mood, it was a bit difficult not to react. Such a shame Jen had turned into one of those people.

I took hold of my suitcase handle and pulled it, stretching it to full length. I really dug the way it did that and wanted to let out a little wee again. Jen hadn't managed to upset me too much, then.

"I doubt I'll see him very often at all," I said, heading for the stairs. "I mean, he'll be working and—"

"It's a good opportunity," she said, following me downstairs.

My suitcase bumped onto every step. "For what?" I didn't dare to turn around and look at her. She'd always been able to read me so well. I couldn't have her spotting some expression on my face that told her I was keeping things from her. Knowing that I was was bad enough—her finding out for sure wasn't something I wanted to entertain. Yet.

"For getting into his pants," she said.

I almost blurted out that I'd been in his pants already but caught myself just in time. And very nice it was inside there too. "God, Jen, wouldn't that be the best thing? Can't see it happening, though. We're friends. He's not interested in me for anything like that."

Liar. Such a bare-faced liar.

"I think you're wrong. He's been looking at you a lot lately."

"Really? I hadn't noticed." At the bottom of the stairs, I reached for the door then pulled it open. Out on the chilly street, I prayed she'd give up this particular conversation. It could only lead to me revealing things.

"Well, he has." She stood beside me, pulling the door closed. "What time's your train?"

I shoved the sleeve of my coat up my arm a bit so I could glance at my watch. "In half an hour. Plenty of time to walk to the station."

I smiled at her, hoping she wasn't going to make our goodbye awkward like she had last night. She'd been drunk and had hung onto me, telling me she'd miss me. I'd thought that was the end of it, yet here we were...

"I'll walk with you, see you off," she said. "As you know, I don't start work until ten."

So she *had* gotten up early on purpose. Did she suspect me and Leon? Did she want to check that I really was going away alone?

My stomach plummeted. Leon was meeting me at the station entrance and I was to hop into his car and we'd go from there. If Jen came along...

"No, no," I said. "I told myself when I got up that my journey of self-discovery" —I tinkled out a laugh and hoped it hadn't sounded as fake as I thought it had—"would start from the minute I woke up. So I'll go by myself. Begin this trip as I mean to go on."

She was hurt, I could tell by the look on her face, but I had to get rid of her.

"All right then." She sighed dramatically.

She gave me a hug that felt awkward then stepped back. I inhaled deeply, telling myself not to give in, not to tell her anything, to stick to the plan.

"I've been seeing Gary," she said. "And I hate myself for not telling you sooner but I didn't want to have to come to you red-faced if it all went wrong. But it hasn't, and everything's lovely—he's lovely—and we're thinking of moving in together. I'm sorry I didn't tell you but—"

"But that's wonderful," I said. "Really lovely. And so you should keep things to yourself sometimes. It's only right when you're in a relationship, isn't it? To have secrets you don't share with anyone else?"

"I suppose, but we always share everything and I've felt such a cow because I haven't. You know, shared." She dipped her head and kicked at a stone on the pavement.

"Listen," I said, "we'll talk about this when I get back—if you want to share then. I really have to go, but I'm excited for you. Really excited. You've fancied him for such a long time."

"I know." She reached out and put her hand on my arm. "And it's just… I want you to have the same thing with Leon."

I already have, love…

Tears pricked the backs of my eyes, damn them.

She smiled. "And I hope you two can, you know, get something going while you're away."

"That would be nice," I said, taking a step away, walking backwards, "and you never know, wonders might happen. See you soon!"

I scurried off with my wonderfully spotty suitcase following faithfully behind, and I didn't stop until I reached the bank where there was a pelican crossing. Some men were inside, about four of them wearing bobble hats, not unusual given the state of the weather. They were waiting in the queue behind a woman—*is that the barmaid from The Rusty Nail?*—who appeared to be holding a week's worth of takings in a gray cloth bag.

Recognition hit me—Cauli was one of the men in the line, I'd know his frame anywhere—and I crossed the road in order to get going in case he turned and saw me. Once on the other side, I looked back at Jen. She stood out in that red coat of hers, scarf flapping like a pennant. She was waving, a smile brightening her face, and the backs of my eyes burned again. She was such a dear friend and deserved all the happiness she'd get by being with Gary. Things were moving on for both of us—and in a very good direction. I waved back then pressed on, my mission to reach the station the only thing that concerned me now.

However, as I was wont to do when going away, I went through my mental checklist. I hadn't used the iron so didn't have images of my flat burning down floating through my head. I hadn't eaten yet either, had only made a cup of tea, so the cooker wasn't an issue and I always turned the kettle off at the wall after use. I hadn't done that this morning, though, being quiet because of waking Jen. Shit, it would be okay, wouldn't it? Things being plugged in had me thinking of my hair straighteners. They were in my suitcase. What was next? The door, I'd definitely locked the door—I remembered how my keys had sounded when they'd gone into my bag. So what was wrong?

The entrance to the station was up ahead. I decided I was doing my usual and worrying about nothing so walked on, quickening my pace in my excitement to see Leon and begin our sordid week away. I entered the station foyer with its white tiled floor and glass dome for a roof. Something popped and I jumped, wondering what the hell it was. It had sounded like a car exhaust backfiring and, telling myself that was the case, I reversed against the wall to wait for Leon to pull up outside. I'd be able to see him through the glass in the door.

The door was pushed open so hard it crashed against the wall. Two of the men from the bank came in and strode toward the stairs that led to platform two. People milling about turned to stare then went about their business once they saw nothing much was going on. I held my breath, wondering when Cauli was going to turn up, then there he was, breezing past me, his hat skew-whiff, half covering one eye. He didn't look in my direction, and I let out a sigh of relief. The last thing I wanted was a confrontation with him to spoil my day.

Leon pulled up outside. My heart thudded hard and I left the station to rush out to him. I glanced up the street, glad that I couldn't see Jen. He took my case, stowed it in the boot, then got into the car at the same time I did. We'd talked about this—no kiss of greeting out in the street. If we were spotted by anyone we knew, I was to say he'd texted me at the last minute to offer me a ride to Blackpool.

As he peeled the car away from the curb and into a slow-moving stream of traffic, he said, "Morning, beautiful."

I smiled, my whole body warming from his words. "Morning to you too. Get away okay?"

"Yep. Gary questioned me last night, but then he knows what's what with us. Only thing is, I'd have thought he'd have told Jen by now, seeing as they're together."

"Weird that he hasn't." I dropped my handbag into the footwell. "Then again, he might have. She caught me as I was leaving this morning. Offered to come to the station with me. Maybe she was testing to see if I'd let anything slip."

"Bloody hell. That was close," he said.

"It was. I mean, she said goodbye last night and I'd thought—"

"No," he said. "I didn't mean her seeing you. That cop car just then. Bloody nearly crashed into us."

I hadn't seen one. I'd been so wrapped up in being with Leon that I hadn't looked outside the car since we'd gotten in. "Probably something and nothing. Still, none of our business. It's our time now. We've been looking forward to this for ages."

Leon reached across to squeeze my thigh. "We have. Be nice, won't it?"

I nodded, wishing he could stop the car and kiss me silly. "Be even nicer when we get back and tell everyone. It'll save so much faffing around."

I'd grown tired of waiting until everyone had left the pub before I could meet up with him. At times I'd even gone home, waited for Jen to go inside her flat, then scarpered back downstairs to meet Leon. Quick lunches in breaks at work and fumbles in his car afterwards. Me returning in the early hours, hoping

Jen didn't get woken up as I went inside. Things could be out in the open, and now Jen had confessed to being with Gary, all we had to do was find a woman for Marshall and we'd be set.

Leon maneuvered onto the road that led out of the city. Excitement kicked up a notch or two—*we're here, doing this, really doing this!*—and I glanced across at him. "I love you, you know."

"I know," he said, giving me a quick glance too then focusing back on the road. "And I've been thinking about when we get back. Where we'll live. Mine or yours."

"I'd prefer a new place myself." I thought of house-hunting together and all the fun it would entail. "It'd be better, don't you think? Us being somewhere we've both chosen. I imagine we'll settle faster that way, none of that 'This is my place and you're encroaching on it' business."

"I wouldn't think like that, but I know what you mean. We'll discuss it more when we get home, shall we?"

I nodded then sighed as my phone started ringing. I'd let my family know I'd be away and not to contact me, so the only person I could imagine would be calling was Jen. Why she couldn't text I didn't know, and I dug my phone out of my bag with a touch of irritation.

The caller display showed her name.

"Hi, Jen," I said, injecting as much friendliness into my voice as I could.

"Oh, thank fuck for that," she said. "Thank *God* you're all right!"

"Of course I'm all right. I'm on the train."

"Oh no. No. You can't be. Get off. Bloody get off as soon as you can. At the next station."

"What the hell for?" I frowned, looking at Leon and rolling my eyes. Why couldn't I just go away without any hassle?

"Because there was a robbery at the bank when you left me. I'm outside — saw the men leaving after they'd shot that barmaid from the pub. You know the one, her with the mad red hair."

"What?" My body went cold.

Leon squeezed my thigh again and I rested my hand on top of his. The contact was reassuring but it didn't take the shock away. It didn't seem possible that just ten minutes ago I'd seen the barmaid in the bank queue.

"Is she okay?" I asked.

"Well, I'm outside the bank now, and from what I can gather she's alive. But that isn't what's worrying me. You are. There were four men, right, and only three got away. I was earwigging at a convo going on between two coppers. The one caught inside the bank started talking straight away, gave the names of his mates and everything. The other three are on the bloody train. To *Blackpool!*"

Lying and keeping secrets had led to lying some more. I didn't like it but had to do it. "It's fine, Jen. Honestly, there's no one on here who looks remotely like a bank robber. I'm in a carriage full of women, in the quiet section. Which is why I really ought to get off the phone. The others are either working or reading."

"But they might come to your carriage," she said. "You're not safe!"

"So I'll get off at the next station."

"What if they hijack the sodding train and you can't get off? Mandy, I'm shitting myself here. I don't know what I'd do without you."

Something scuffed across the mouthpiece at her end, material from her jacket, I assumed.

"Hang on a second," she whispered. "They're bringing the caught man out. Oh my God, this is insane!" A pause, then, "Mandy. Mandy, it's one of the men from the pub last night. The visiting rugby team!"

Even though I was sitting, my legs went to jelly. I felt sick and opened my mouth to answer her but couldn't form any words. I'd seen them in the queue — *seen them!* — and Cauli had gone past me at the station.

"Blimey," I managed. "I saw them. At the station. I just assumed they'd be going home."

"Well, they're trying to, obviously but... Hold on." Another pause. "I just heard a copper say they're not stopping the train until the police are in place farther up the line. Mandy, you *have* to be careful!"

I swallowed. I couldn't do this any longer. Couldn't let her think I was in danger. "Jen, listen to me. I can't go into it now, but I'm not on the train, okay? I lied. You don't have to worry — I'm not on it. I'll tell you what's going on when I get back, just not now. I love you to bits but I have to go."

I cut the call then switched my phone off, not wanting the third degree. Guilt arrived, as I'd known it would, and I babbled what she'd told me to Leon.

"She'll be fine now she knows you're safe," he said. "But fucking hell, if I'd have known why those men were really here... I shoved him about last night. He could have turned nasty."

"He could have but didn't." I thought of Cauli calling me a bitch. Of how things between us could have gone down a completely different route. I shuddered and pushed him from my mind.

No one was going to spoil this holiday. No one.

Chapter Four

We stood outside the hotel. It was called Smithin Lodge but didn't resemble one. It was the same as any other seaside effort, really, all light-blue paint and hundreds of windows. A load of square eyes, that's what they looked like — the black sills reminded me of kohl liner, the overhangs of black scalloped wood at the tops the mascara-laden lashes.

It wasn't anything special, just an average place that would serve our needs well enough. We walked through the glass double doors and into a foyer that smelled of whatever had recently been served for lunch. Fish and chips, I thought. Leon checked us in, trying to calm a very stressed receptionist who couldn't seem to find our details. She had irate brown hair that stood up in long tufts where she may or may not have scrunched it in her fists in frustration. She appeared to have had a bloody bad day so far and I was glad I wasn't the one dealing with her.

We'd been sent a little booking package through the post — a map of Blackpool, our printed-out receipt, and a selection of leaflets — which had gone some way to making this trip away seem more real. Now that we were here I could hardly believe it.

Ahead was a large white desk shaped like an S with a bunch of flowers on top that had seen better days. They were pink and yellow roses, drooping, and I fancied I looked the same, a bit wilted and tired. The journey had been long with a stop along the way at the services — a petrol station as well as a WHSmiths, KFC and toilet facilities in one sectioned-off building. I'd been almost wetting myself by the time we'd gotten there — drinking Diet Coke had done that — and I'd had to queue for a cubicle, which hadn't helped matters. Braiding my legs wasn't a skill I was good at. It had been surprisingly busy. People had milled about here, there and everywhere, and I'd wondered if the world and his wife were all on their way to the coast for a bit of R and R.

I turned my head. To the right were two sets of elevator doors, shiny metal that reflected the rest of the foyer. Three chocolate-brown leather sofas had been positioned around a low oak coffee table, which held various magazines in piles that were so straight only someone with OCD could have stacked them. A white Formica shelving unit held pamphlets showing the local attractions. These were slotted haphazardly in places where people had removed them to have a nose then put them back. All in all it was a nice place and I was pleased I'd left the location to Leon. Providing the receptionist found our booking and we got to stay here.

He backed away from the desk, thanking the woman, who patted her red cheeks then waved her hands about in front of them. I could understand if she'd gotten hot and bothered through dealing with him. Leon was quite a bloody gorgeous dish and then some. He swiveled to face me. I almost fanned *my* face. He took my suitcase hostage, tugging it along while carrying his manly black one as we walked to the elevators. I liked the fact that him being seen tugging a spotty pink case didn't bother him.

"Not too shabby," he said, nodding to indicate the lobby, "and the pool's heated apparently."

"Lovely."

"Did you bring a swim suit?" he asked.

"I did. A bikini. God help your poor eyes when you see me in it."

"Stop saying things like that. You'll look lovely. I forgot mine. And no, I didn't mean my bikini, before you say it."

I laughed, imagining him wearing one. "What happened back there, at the desk?"

"Oh, she had my name under something else, simple spelling mistake. Had me worried for a bit, though. Made me think our little jaunt away might be spoiled from the start."

"It already was with Jen catching me on the landing then that bank robbery. But nothing else will go wrong now, you'll see." I hoped that would turn out to be true.

He pressed the elevator button on the wall and I thought of how that finger had pressed my button more times than I could count.

"Ooh, here it is," I said, excited at the prospect of seeing our room. Our little den of sin.

The doors opened to the sound of a loud *ding*, and we stepped on, lady before gentleman. I smiled, knowing I was no lady but grateful for Leon's manners all the same. He'd said once that I was his princess and that he'd do anything to make me happy. So far he'd been telling the truth. I couldn't imagine being without him now, and the thought of us moving in together was the stuff made of girly dreams. No more poky little flat. No more waking up alone. And wouldn't it be nice to be woken up with a cup of tea in bed instead of having to stagger into the kitchen to make it myself?

Life was going to be so good.

The doors closed and I reached across to stroke his hand.

"Is it mad to be this excited?" I asked. "About going away with a man? It's like we're being really naughty."

"That was the idea, wasn't it?" He kissed my cheek. "To act as though we were having an affair, that we shouldn't really be here?"

"It was."

I looked at the numbers beside the buttons on the wall lighting up one after the other. The elevator lurched to a stop at the seventh floor, and the doors slid open to reveal a cream-painted corridor with a patterned carpet the color of babies' poo. Nice…

I stepped out and waited for Leon, who led the way to room seventy. I went inside first, pleased to see what our money had paid for—I'd insisted on going Dutch.

A double bed with wooden cabinets either side stood against the wall to our right, and a door there led to a small but clean bathroom. A huge window was ahead, dressed with heavy blue curtains and a frilly pelmet, the material a match for the quilt cover. The floor was tiled cream—something I hadn't encountered in a British hotel before—but other than that it resembled any other holiday residence I'd been in.

"This is nice," I said, imagining us on the bed, tangled up in that quilt, all hot and sweaty. "Glad that gross carpet isn't in here. And the bed looks comfy."

Leon set the bags down, closed the door, then came up to me. He drew me close, held me firm with one hand at the bottom of my back, and stroked my cheek.

"This has been a long time coming," he said. "Us two gadding about in secret was fun for a while but I just want you to myself with no worries about who sees us."

I knew exactly how he felt. "Do you think we'll get on? You know, now we'll spend more time together? Snatched meetings where we've shagged for most of it... We haven't exactly got to know each other's quirks, have we, apart from the ones we show in public when we're with the others in the pub."

"Nope, but we've got time to get to know them now. And whatever yours are, I'll love them." He smiled. "Or put up with them because I can't imagine doing anything else."

I swatted his chest. "Cheeky sod. You say it like you haven't got any quirks of your own. For all I know you could leave blobs of toothpaste in the sink or your hairs when you've had a shave."

"You mean that's a problem if I do?" He widened his eyes.

"It might be. You'll have to wait to find out whether I turn into the dragon from hell when I spot things like that. Or if you ball your socks when you take them off, leaving me to unravel them before I put them in the washer. Now that? Mmm, I could kill for a lesser offense."

He laughed, a bit unsure, I fancied.

He looked at me, maybe working out whether I'd meant what I'd said. "But you'll forgive all my quirks because, let's face it, you can't get enough of me."

I chuckled at his serious expression. He laughed again too then tugged me over to the bed. We flopped onto it, bouncing with the mattress, and he gathered me in his arms. God, I felt so safe, so wanted, and so bloody free. Like I had no worries and all that mattered was being with him like this.

I toed off my shoes and studied him. He was all manly and handsome, his dark hair shorter from a recent cut, stubble darkening his jaw. I could eat him all up.

"We should unpack and go sightseeing," I said, knowing we wouldn't. I got off the bed and stood beside it.

"We should." He joined me and undid the top button of my shirt. "But I'd rather unpack you."

He continued with my buttons until my shirt gaped open, revealing a boring, lacy white bra. The underwire accentuated the swells, and he eyed them, licking his lips.

"I can taste them already," he said, flicking his gaze back to my face. Then he lowered it again, much farther down. "And taste *that*."

My cunt ached in response and I swallowed words that waited to be spoken. I didn't want to spoil the moment with anything that might come out. A flippant sentence, something inappropriate. Something silly.

"And *that* tastes beautiful," he said, undoing my jeans then sliding them down my legs.

On his knees, he tapped my ankle for me to lift my leg. I did, first one then the other, and stood before him in just my underwear. He reached up for my knickers, dragging them down, discarding them after they'd been removed.

"This," he said, "is what I want to taste. You. Your cream."

I shuddered with need, with the expectation of him burying his face in my cunt and making me come with his tongue. He glided his hands up my inner thighs, asserting pressure at the top so I widened my legs. And bury his face he did, sucking, licking. He massaged my arse cheeks and pulled me closer. I rested my hands on his head, closed them into fists around his hair, dared to push so he was closer still. He worked magic with his tongue, sliding it up and down then around my clit, circles that teased but didn't give me exactly what I needed. I let out a whimper, keen to have him assault my clit all out, flattening his tongue and swiping there over and over until pleasure erupted.

"I need to come already," I said, the excitement of it too much, him down there on his knees, servicing me.

He paused, reared back an inch or two, breath hot on my flesh. He stood then, taking me in his arms to place me on the bed. He climbed on, the opposite way to me, positioning himself so his cock was at my mouth and his mouth was at my cunt. My stomach muscles did a little dance, then my tummy rolled, me needing, really needing him to lower his head and lick my cunt.

I stared at his cock, at his balls, and reached up to take hold of him at his base. I guided his dick to my mouth, licking the end, swirling my tongue around it then plunging him inside. As I created suction, he dove onto my cunt, kissing and laving while I sucked. Both of us tending to the other at the same time sent my head spinning, the pleasure I got from giving him a blow job rivalling that between my legs.

I groaned, the sound buzzing around his cock and on my tongue. He groaned back, lowering himself, pushing deeper into my mouth. I took him all, his tip right to the back of my throat. I lifted one hand to part his arse cheeks and used the finger of my other to circle his pucker. He licked me faster, and I took that to mean what I was doing to him was turning him on. I moaned around his cock again as a streak of bliss shot right up inside me, spreading everywhere, the center of the pleasure anchored at my clit. He flickered his tongue over it, ramping up my desire, and I lifted my hips, wanting pressure, friction, pressure.

I sucked harder, lifting my head then lowering it at a languid pace, while he treated me to more frantic movement. It was too much—his cock in my mouth, my cunt against his—and I writhed as his dick throbbed on my tongue. I closed my eyes. My toes scrunched and my cunt contracted of their own accord. I widened my legs, bent them at the knees, and he curled his arm around one thigh to plunge his fingers into my pussy.

I came, humping his face, rubbing my wet flesh against him, sucking his cock until I tasted pre-cum. He erupted, spunk flooding my mouth, and I swallowed the first expulsion, waiting for the second. My orgasm rioted, wreaking havoc, crashing me this way and that. Another shot of cum hit the back of my throat, and I swallowed again, relaxing my suction and easing him out a little so the third shot would coat my tongue. It did, just as I shuddered through the final throes of pleasure. I slathered his cum on his dick then licked it off. He French kissed my flesh, softly, the aftershocks less spiky owing to his attention. I let myself relax, sink into the bed, trailing my fingertips down his sides as far as I could reach. He stopped kissing there to peck my inner thighs, then shifted forward so his cock left my mouth.

Moving to rest beside me, he took me in his arms, both of us on our sides. He threw one of his legs over me, ensuring I couldn't move—I didn't want to, could have stayed there forever—and played his fingertips up and down my back. I did the same to him, twirling one finger in his hair each time my hand reached the top. This was...this was as close to Heaven as I was going to get.

"Christ," he said. "It just gets better every time."

"Mmm." I snuggled my cheek closer to his chest.

"We just fit, don't we?"

"We do. We're like a finished Rubik's Cube. All the colors in the right places, all our sides complete."

"We should put it back in the box, then, so no one can come along and mess it up." He played with my hair. "I don't want anyone playing with you."

"I feel the same. I don't want anyone else playing with me either."

He laughed. "You were supposed to say you wouldn't want anyone else playing with *me*."

"I know, but I thought I'd tease. And no, I most definitely do *not* want anyone playing with you. Only me. That's all you have now, just me. How does that prospect grab you?"

"By the balls—in a good way."

I stopped caressing his back and tunneled my hand between us. Cupped his balls. "And these aren't for anyone else." I moved my hand to his cock. "Or this."

"I promise you, the thought of anyone else touching them now..."

"You mean you've thought about that?" I smiled.

"Well, no, but I'm just saying, the thought—"

I laughed, lifting my head to look at him. "You're so easy to wind up." I squeezed his cock a bit. "And get hard again."

He pushed me onto my back, straddling me, pinning my wrists to the bed above my head. "You little…"

I laughed again, giddy with happiness—until he silenced me with a very hot and *very* cunt-tingling kiss.

Chapter Five

We'd eaten dinner in the hotel restaurant—nothing fancy, just fish and chips with mushy peas—and had walked the long road toward the Pleasure Beach, which was open until eight. It was six now, so there was plenty of time to have a look around. I wasn't sure I wanted to do anything much inside. I'd never been a speed freak so the rollercoasters or other fast rides didn't appeal. I *did* like the atmosphere of theme parks and fairs, though, and watching other people having fun made me feel light and happy.

I anticipated a good evening.

It was colder here than at home, and I supposed it would be, seeing as we were right on the coast. The whoosh of the sea had the hairs on my neck standing on end, and I had to force myself not to listen because the ocean had always scared me. We tagged on to the back of a short queue and I smiled at three children who were there with their mum and dad, I presumed, jumping up and down and chattering about what they wanted to go on. I thought of what I'd said to Jen about me reliving the past, and a slew of memories from holidays gone by swept through my head. I smiled wider, remembering how I'd sat in our caravan once and had imagined living there all by myself, keeping 'house' and playing with my dolls as though they were real babies.

Would that couple be me and Leon in years to come? Would we have kids and bring them here, telling them we'd visited Blackpool before they'd even been a twinkle in our eyes? I couldn't imagine it but hoped our future held all the usual things most women yearned for. Love, marriage, a house, kids, a stinky dog or snooty-looking cat…

The queue moved up. The children squealed and clapped. Their turn came to be served, and after they'd gone through the turnstile I lost sight of them in the crowd. We paid the entry fee after waiting in a surprisingly long line. I had the feeling many locals came here at night as some of them didn't look that excited. The night air had a nip to it, but I was bundled up in a warm coat and scarf. Leon had a black padded bomber jacket on and a dark gray beanie hat.

We had a wander, arm in arm. This was the life, with no particular place to be and no constraints on time. It seemed alien not being constantly glued to my phone, too, which I hadn't turned on since speaking to Jen. No texts, calls or Facebook for me this week. Leon had opted to do the same. He'd said he didn't want disturbing.

There were several rollercoasters, all of them big and long, the people on them screaming their heads off. I was thankful, after having had two glasses of wine with dinner, that we'd chosen not to go on any of them. I didn't fancy the result—or the insane picture the camera would undoubtedly catch. And Leon would insist on buying it, showing it to our gang. Me with my mouth wide open, other than to take in his cock, wasn't something I relished.

"As fun as it looks," I said, "I'm not the Mad Mandy everyone thinks. I like the idea of keeping my feet on the ground."

"Be a laugh if all of us came up here, though. I'd love to watch Jen and Gary shitting themselves on that bugger. It's massive."

The rollercoaster in question appeared a bit rickety to me. I shuddered. "It doesn't look safe. And it's too high. I hate that feeling you get just before the car goes over the first dip. Last time I went on one I was sick once I got off."

"Poor you. Hey, look. Maybe we could get married here."

He pointed to a section on one of the leaflets he'd picked up after we'd paid to get in. Apparently, they held wedding ceremonies and the receptions in The Horseshoe, Paradise Room, White Tower or Attic. I couldn't imagine doing that, having a wedding inside a theme park, but for now that wasn't what stood out in my mind. The fact that he'd mentioned marriage was.

"Married?" I asked.

"Something to aim toward, isn't it? If you want to, that is." He gave me a sheepish grin, as though he'd been caught with his thoughts projected from his head onto a large screen live on air.

"I do," I said. "It's just that I hadn't realized you —"

Someone hefty bumped into me, jarring me sideways. I lost my balance and squealed, the kind of squeal all women tend to make — *whoop!* — before giggling and going red in the face. I reached out for Leon, who grabbed me just before I managed to make a prat of myself and fall to the ground. My shoulder hurt from the barge, a flaring ache that throbbed quite a bit before petering out. Indignant, I swirled to give the person what for.

"Hey," Leon shouted at the retreating person, a broad-shouldered, tall man.

"Leave it," I said, taking hold of his hand. Now that I'd seen who had barreled into us, I wasn't sure admonishing him was a good idea. "It doesn't matter, and getting into a fight with a bloke that size—"

Another man breezed past, and I turned to see where they'd been and what they were running from. All I could see was a stall where huge, neon-colored teddy bears were the prizes.

A third streaked toward us, balaclava over his face, eyes a pair of staring menaces through the holes. My stomach churned, fear making my palms sweat. There was something about this man that upset my chakra or whatever the hell it was called. What was going on, and who wore balaclavas over their faces other than when committing crime or going skiing? It wasn't *that* cold tonight. I felt sick at the fast flicker of bad thoughts running around in my head.

Committing crime…

Leon and I sidestepped at the same time—in opposite directions. The man headed straight for us, smacking into our still linked hands, and went hurtling over our arms, hitting the concrete forehead first. That had to have hurt. I squealed, more for the pain he'd be going through than anything else. It was like watching *You've Been Framed.*

If I'd had my phone on in time I could have filmed that and made two hundred and fifty quid.

I released Leon's hand to place mine over my mouth. I was torn between laughing through fear and crying. The man let out a growl of frustration and scrabbled to his feet, turning to glare at us while wiping grit from his hands onto his jeaned thighs.

"You," he said, pointing at me. "And you. What's the fucking deal? You following me or what?"

The rasp in his voice clicked on my recognition switch and reminded me of someone else. Someone not very pleasant and who might well have committed a crime back home lately, except he'd worn a bobble hat on that occasion.

"Oh, shit," I whispered, lowering my hands and moving closer to Leon.

"Following you?" Leon asked. "I don't bloody think so, mate, and watch where you're going, all right?"

I wanted to tell Leon to be quiet. What was he playing at, talking back to a man who clearly wasn't the law-abiding kind? Instead, I stood beside him and squeezed his hand in warning. I just had to hope he took the hint and didn't think I'd done it from simply being frightened. He stared at the man for what seemed a long time, then Cauli—yes, I'd swear it was him—turned and ran off.

The man shouted back, "If I see you again, you'd better fucking watch yourself!"

I didn't like the sound of that. A threat, that's what it had been, right in the middle of a family theme park. What the world was coming to I didn't know.

We turned to continue walking the park, and I wondered if Leon shooting at targets to win me an ugly teddy might make him feel better. A middle-aged, balding security guard barged along then, his momentum so quick we were left jostled in his wake.

"What the fuck is it with this place?" Leon said, tugging me close. "You okay?"

"Yes, but... That man? He was that dickhead from The Rusty Nail. The one who might have robbed the bank. Didn't you recognize his voice?" Once I'd said it out loud it seemed to make it more real. I hadn't been imagining it—it *had* been him, otherwise, why would he ask if we'd been following him? My legs weakened and I leaned harder into Leon to steady myself. I felt sick, what with my head spinning from more than just the two glasses of wine. I looped my arm into the crook of his elbow so I had something to hold on to. Thank goodness my anchor was there. If this had happened when I'd been on my own...

"Fucking hell, Mandy. We come away and a bit of home follows us. Typical." Leon led me to a bench close to the teddy stall and urged me to sit. "Do you want me to get you a coffee or something? There's a van over there, look. And d'you reckon we ought to ring the police?"

I thought about that—had thought about it while we'd traveled up here too—but really, I knew nothing that could be of any help to the police, apart from knowing where a criminal was. All Cauli had done was approach me in a pervy way at the pub and expect me to fall at his feet. I didn't know him, could only do one of those e-fit picture things, and to be honest, I didn't fancy it. Besides, if they'd shot the barmaid in the bank—why the hell would I want to get involved further?

What if they shot me?

"No," I said. "Best to keep out of it. He recognized us. We could get hurt..." I rested my head on his shoulder and shivered. The night air had cooled the bench and the chill was seeping through my jeans. "What gets me, is why are they here if they've just got away with robbing a bank? Shouldn't they be hiding out or whatever it is robberish people do?"

"You'd think so." Leon stared into the distance.

I followed suit, attention on the glittering lights of Blackpool Tower, and wished we'd gone to Paris instead. No one would have disturbed us there. We could have had a really romantic holiday, without anyone we knew literally bumping into us.

It felt odd to be sitting inside a theme park just staring, not going on any rides or playing hook the duck—if they even had that here. We could have sat on the promenade and saved the entry fee, probably watched the rollercoasters from there. The buzz had gone out of the evening for me, exchanged with the sting of fear and the desire to go back to the hotel where we'd be safe. Then my imagination ran away with me. What if Cauli was outside, waiting for us to leave? What if *he* followed *us* and found out where we were staying?

A knot of tension settled in my temples, and I snuggled even closer to Leon. "I'm a bit scared now."

"Maybe we should stay in the hotel all week. Get room service, not leave until it's time to go home," he said.

"That might be a good idea," I said.

"Then again," he went on, "we've already talked about what we wanted to see and do while we were here. Much as I'd like to stay in bed with you for a whole week, we're meant to be having fun *outside* the sheets. That was the point, wasn't it? To get to know one another better in other ways?"

It was, and I nodded. "Yes, but we can still have sex. We're meant to be acting like we're having an illicit affair—and who has one of those without getting their jollies? Forget I said anything about being scared. I'm just being silly, thinking of if we see that man again. That's twice now in one day. What are the odds? Not only did they supposedly rob a bank back home, but they just happened to escape to the same place we were going. A massive coincidence, granted, but it's still unnerving. I thought that kind of shit only happened in books and films."

I paused to take a breath. "And we don't even know if they live here or whether this is just a stop-off point while they do whatever else it is they'd planned to do, if they were even doing anything." I felt a babble coming on. "And of course they've planned to do something—or have done already—otherwise, why the hell were they running through here? And him with a thiefy balaclava on. And us not knowing our way round here, so if they ambush us and take us somewhere we won't know how to get away or where to escape to. "

"When you put it like that... Bloody hell, it sounds mad. Come on. We'll have a bit of a walk round, calm down, and if you're still edgy later we'll go back to the hotel. A good night's sleep will help then we can have the holiday we wanted, starting in the morning."

As we rose to continue our tour of the park, a security guard approached us, complete with Magnum, P.I. mustache and a Colombo wonky eye. It added to the weirdness of the evening and I shirked off yet another shiver. The only things missing on him were a Hawaiian shirt and beige raincoat. And didn't one of them smoke a cigar?

"Excuse me," he said. "Could you come with me for a moment, please?"

I gripped Leon's arm. I didn't want to go with the guard but doubted we'd have much choice. I had no idea if they had the same powers as the police. And seeing as we were on property they were supposed to protect. Yes, we'd go with them. Surely it would only be to answer a few questions.

"Okay," I said, glancing up at Leon.

We followed the guard to what appeared to be a blank wall painted with jungle-like scenery. Something for the kiddies to look at, I supposed. The guard placed his hand on a tree trunk, and a door swung inwards, revealing nothing but blackness inside. I waited for him to say "After you!" and prepared myself to respond with "Not on your Nelly!" but he went in first. A light came on, and we stood in the doorway to a room that had a wooden desk against the far wall and white worktops like those in a kitchen attached to three of the four walls. Large monitors sat on top of them, each screen split into four sections and showing a different location in the park.

"You can leave the door ajar," he said. "My colleague will be along in a minute. It's just that I saw that man talking to you when he'd fallen over. I'll need to ask you about that."

So we weren't going to be able to get away without speaking to someone in authority about Cauli after all. I was irritated by this turn of events. What was supposed to be a saucy holiday getting to know my secret boyfriend better was rapidly turning into a people-doing-illegal-things affair.

The balding guard from five minutes ago dove in, startling the shit out of me so that I let out another of those stupid little *whoops*. He shut the door. His face was red from exertion, and he breathed with a wheeze that whistled, reminding me of a referee in a football match.

"Bloody got out," he said between pants, sweat dribbling down his temples. "All three of them. Ned at the gate let them through, yet I'd radioed him to say they were going to try to leave." He bent over and braced himself with his hands on his knees. "If I didn't know better I'd say he knew something. Like he'd ignored me and let them out on purpose. Mayday, mayday, I'd said, but he reckoned it didn't come through. My arse."

I glanced from one guard to the other. Cauli was out there somewhere, just like I'd imagined he would be. I closed my eyes for a second or two to steady my nerves. Opening them, I said, "What did you need to know?" I wanted to get out of there as quickly as possible. "Only we came in to the park late so don't have much time left. And we *won't* be coming here again."

Magnum came up to us, notebook in sausage-fingered hand. He squinted in a Columbo manner. "What did he say to you?"

Leon began, "He asked us if we—"

"Made a habit of getting in people's way," I said. "He was annoyed he'd tripped over us, that's all."

I didn't look at Leon. If I did, he'd silently question me as to why I'd lied. We'd look like we were hiding something and more questions would follow.

"I see, and that was all?" Magnum scribbled in his notebook.

"Yes. Then he ran off." I chewed my bottom lip.

Magnum sighed. "Right. Well, it was worth a try. Might have gotten something worth following up on. As it is, they've got away with a valuable piece of jewelry that had been loaned to a bride for her wedding day. I said it was stupid to have her wearing it, didn't I?" he said, turning to his bald co-worker. "But no one listened to me, as usual." His mustache rippled.

I smiled. "Well, um, we'd really like to get going now? I want to tour the park at least once before it closes."

Magnum sighed and tweaked his life-of-its-own mustache. "Yes, yes, sorry to have troubled you."

We escaped back into the park, and I tugged Leon away from the jungle wall before I spoke. "I wasn't going to tell them Cauli recog—"

"Who?" Leon frowned.

"Cauli. You know, Cauliflower Ears. Rugby player. That's my little name for him."

"I see."

"I wasn't going to tell them he'd recognized us. I don't want to get involved—and I'd rather we stay in here and look about for a while in case Cauli's outside somewhere. You just don't know, do you, how people like him work."

"No," Leon said, taking hold of my hand. "And as for stealing jewelry. Fucking hell, what have we walked into?"

"I don't know—and I don't want to. Let's forget this. Just…oh, kiss me will you? Make all this go away."

Chapter Six

Leon took me in his arms and kissed me senseless. I held onto the front of his jacket, my head going giddy. I was aware of a couple of people letting out loud whoops owing to the show we were putting on but didn't care. I just wanted contact, some form of normality, something to blot the sense of nervousness out.

If only it were that easy.

He broke away and looked at me, giving me the kind of visual examination that meant he was checking to see if I needed some kind of reassurance. I'd felt better but a kiss wasn't going to erase the weirdness of what had happened. Even if he told me everything was going to be okay I might not believe him.

I smiled and walked with him to the exit, where we waited for other people to leave before us. The air had a crueler nip to it and the thought of a hot chocolate, flannel pajamas and fluffy slippers was becoming more appealing by the second. We had quite a long walk to our hotel, though, so any chance of getting warm meant walking with Leon's arm around my shoulders, me pressed close to his side. My breath left me in puffs of gray smoke, and a fleeting memory came again of me as a child, blowing air out and pretending I was smoking a cigarette. Thank goodness I'd never started that habit. If I had, I'd have chuffed through a packet of twenty after what had gone on this evening.

Outside the Pleasure Beach, I scanned the street one way then the other. My heart was being put through the wringer, what with it beating so fast, and I took a couple of deep breaths to steady my nerves.

There were quite a few people milling around or walking from the park and back into Blackpool proper so that it was difficult to see if Cauli was hanging about. I got a shudder down my spine nonetheless, as though my senses knew he was there but I didn't. Where could he be hiding anyway if not among the crowds? I looked again, harder this time, and, definitely not seeing him, told myself I ought to stop worrying. What kind of man would remain at the scene of a crime and risk being caught anyway?

A madman.

I shuddered again.

"Come on," Leon said. "We should go. Get back to the hotel and put this behind us."

We headed down the street, me keeping ultra aware. No one seemed weird or to be lurking. I relaxed a bit. The scent of the sea wafted over me on a hefty breeze, and I stared out at it, reluctant to do so but knowing that if I wanted to get over my phobia of it I had to. It was rough and appeared so black, the crests of the choppy waves dark gray instead of white. Such a vast thing, the ocean, that the idea of being stranded on it gave me the creeps. I preferred earth beneath my feet, thank you very much, yet the horrid feeling of literally being lost out at sea either on a boat or in the water was a strong one. I likened it to our current situation. We were out of our depth with this Cauli business. We didn't mix with people like that, only ever read of such things in the newspapers, so to have the fingertips of crime poking us was unnerving and something I wished we'd never experienced. And with his last threat still ringing in my ears...

"I'm still a bit scared," I blurted, turning from the sea to focus ahead. "In case he comes back and gets us anyway, whether he sees us and thinks we've been following him or not. And what if we do see him again? It's not like we'll have done it on purpose, is it. He'll think we did, though. What if he turns nasty?"

"He won't—because we won't see him. What are the chances of that, eh?"

"The same as the chances of seeing him here when the last time we'd had contact was at home. More chance, actually."

Bloody hell. Dear God, please don't let us cross paths with him again.

Leon put his arm around my waist and hugged me to his side. "Unless he's on a rampage to rob the good people of Blackpool further, I'd say we just had the misfortune to be in the wrong place at the wrong time. Twice, yes, but—"

"They say things happen in threes, though. What if—"

Leon stopped and cupped my face. "Pack it in, all right?" He kissed the end of my nose and stared into my eyes. "Things will be fine."

I wasn't sure if he was saying it to me as well as to reassure himself. Either way, I felt marginally better and decided it might be preferable if I put these incidents to the back of my mind and tried to enjoy our holiday. It had been tainted by that man even before we'd left for Blackpool, and to let the memory of it linger was something only I had control over. He could only ruin it if I allowed it. The problem was I had a tendency to go over things time and again, to let them manifest into something bigger, scarier, until I imagined being stabbed or shot.

That's enough. Living your life like this isn't good for you. Grow a pair.

"Right," I said, coming to a decision. "We'll go back to the hotel then get ready to do something. Go out, get drunk or whatever, and have a good laugh like we would if we were at home. Fuck Cauli and the scabby donkey he rode in on!"

Just saying that brought a whole new perspective to the fore. Bravery bolstered my spine and calmed my nerves. I was in control of my emotions, no one else.

"That's the way to look at it," Leon said, smiling. "We could do a pub crawl and see who falls down first. They're always fun. And you're hilarious after you've had a few. We can let alcohol take everything away."

He knew me so well. In the past I'd been known to drink all the men in our gang under the table. Leon was issuing a challenge—one he knew he might not win. I smiled and wondered if he'd drink pints of lager or join me on the vodka.

"Only hilarious after I've had a few?" I asked. "Charming, and there's me trying to be funny all the time."

He laughed then we walked in companionable silence. I people-watched, playing the game I usually played with Jen. We'd named it 'What's her Secret?', and we chose a woman to focus on and made up a life we thought suited her. The last time we'd played it was just before I'd shagged Leon for the first time.

A couple ahead were kissing under a streetlamp, showcased as though on stage, the stars of the play. Her long, waist-length hair was amber from the light, swinging a bit from where he may have pulled her into his arms before I'd spotted them. Her two-piece black skirt suit, stockings and high heels seemed at odds with our surroundings. Most people were wearing jeans and fleece jackets or chunky coats. Had she just finished working in an office and had come out to meet him?

He, on the other hand, had opted for jeans and a leather jacket, at ease in his casual get-up. Loose-limbed and with an air about him of not giving a shit, he brought to mind James Dean. I couldn't imagine him wearing a suit, working in the same place she did. He held her as if she were precious, that she might break, and that didn't fit with his bad-boy impression. She clutched him like she never wanted to let him go, reminding me of what I'd thought when I'd looked at the sea. She'd drown without him, that much was plain.

I pressed into Leon a little harder—I'd drown without him too.

He ruffled my hair.

"Me and Jen play this game," I said, explaining it to him. "Want to play?"

"Could do," he said. "Something to do while we're walking."

"That couple there. Under the streetlamp. What do you see?"

It would be interesting to get a man's perspective. I knew Leon was romantic, a different kind of man from any other I'd been with, and the fact that he was prepared to join in on something that might be seen as girly was a bonus in itself.

I was keeping him—forever. Never letting go.

"Two people who are kissing," he said.

He'd need a bit of help getting into this.

I groaned. "Is that all? You don't get anything else? Even something made up?"

A gull swooped down in front of us, beady eyes like Cauli's, its beak open as if it wanted to peck my nose off. Or maybe it wanted to see if we had any chips it could steal. I squealed.

He laughed. "Bloody hell. They're a nuisance, they are."

He led me across the road, and on the other side I admired a horse and carriage that I assumed was used for up-and-down journeys along the seafront. If horses didn't scare me to death I'd have asked Leon if he fancied a trip, but seeing as they did and I wanted to keep my knickers clean, I didn't bother.

"So, the game?" I said. "What can you come up with about that couple?"

"I don't think I'm on the same wavelength as you and Jen, but okay, I'll give it a go. They're having an affair. Is that the way you play it?"

"Yes, go on."

"She's married and has managed to get away for a long weekend. Maybe she's been seeing that man for a while, I don't know."

A gaggle of women came toward us, off their faces on alcohol, on a hen night by the look of them. Their outfits left a lot to be desired, skin on show in abundance, blown-up condoms attached to their scanty dresses. I could see me and Jen doing that. Then I realized it would only be me and her on my hen night—I didn't really have any other female friends—as the others in our gang were male.

"Where did they meet, that couple?" I prompted.

"Online," he said. "On one of those dating agencies. You've seen the adverts for them, right? Uniform dating or whatever. She knew her marriage wasn't going anywhere so signed up for a laugh. Her friends made her do it. Let her sign up using one of their credit cards so she didn't get caught using hers. Umm, let me think. She didn't expect to find someone she clicked with so soon. He's single and spends most of his time tormenting himself that he can't be with her as much as he wants to." He sighed. "I know that feeling."

"Me too, but when we go back home we'll get it all out in the open."

I imagined sitting in The Rusty Nail, around one of the tables, and explaining that we were a couple now. It would change the dynamics of our gang, no doubt about it, and poor Marshall would possibly feel left out if Jen and Gary announced they were also together.

"I wonder," I continued, "whether Marshall's ever thought of an online dating agency."

Leon laughed—hard and loud. "What? Are you kidding? He's too shy for that kind of thing. I mean, look at him. He doesn't approach women, only ever goes out with any if *they* ask *him*. We keep telling him to grow some balls but so far they haven't got any bigger."

"Like you and Gary, you mean? From what I remember, *you* had no balls to ask *me* out. Gary arranged it all for you. The conversation about it before you came round was on Facebook, of all places."

"Shit, that seems like so long ago, doesn't it? Yet it wasn't. Only a few months."

I glanced across at him. He had a wistful look on his face—eyes dreamy, the touch of a smile on his lips. Were memories floating through his mind like they were in mine? I recalled the night we'd finally gotten together. In the Rusty Nail. Leon with a T-shirt held over his head by one of the others, his torso on show. Me going up to him and pretending to be a woman named Pussy Pwoar. I'd gotten my first touch of him then, had rubbed his torso, thinking I'd never get to do it again after that. But later, Gary had brought him round to my flat, Leon blindfolded, me seducing him—or making an effort to anyway. I'd thought he hadn't known it was me yet he had.

Happiness spread through me and I grinned. "A few months of hiding and lying. It was fun, I'll give you that, but enough's enough. But it was bloody good fun. Exciting."

"It was. Best thing that's ever happened to me."

I love you.

"So, you need to finish your 'What's her Secret?' story," I said. "How will it end for them?"

"She's so in love with that man she'll leave her husband. She might not even go back home after this weekend. She has no children so there isn't any need, and she has the kind of job she could transfer easily." He shrugged. "There you go, happily ever after. That do you?"

"That wasn't a bad start. You could get very good at this game."

"I take it you play it often?"

"We used to. Lately, not at all. Seeing as I'll be spending more time with you now instead of Jen, you'll need to prepare yourself for indulging me."

He groaned. "I'll do anything for you."

I giggled and spotted our hotel ahead. I glanced around us, checking to see if we'd been followed. We hadn't as far as I could tell.

A glittering sign for a casino grabbed my attention and all thoughts of Cauli loitering or us getting drunk on a pub crawl went out of my head.

"Shall we go there?" I said, pointing.

"Bloody hell, do you think I'm made of money?" he joked.

"No, but we could play the slots. That won't cost much if we stretch it out over a couple of hours. And we could play 'What's her Secret?' except we're the couple with a made-up life. We can pretend we're rich, that casinos are something we visit all the time. I brought a nice dress with me, and you've got your suit. Come on, what d'you say? Shall we become Mr and Mrs Ponsonby or whatever? Be someone else for the rest of the night?"

"What is it with you and your identities? As if Pussy Pwoar wasn't enough, you're dragging me into being another person with you."

"Aww, come on. It'll be fun, I promise."

"Fuck it, go on then."

I squealed like a silly girl and tugged him into our hotel. The warmth hit me and began defrosting my face. A crowd stood in front of the elevators—men in suits—and we stood behind them. The doors of one opened, the men got in and, while we waited for the second lift, I thought about how to style my hair in order to make me appear rich and classy. I would be a lady of leisure, while Leon would be a banker or a lawyer, keeping me in the lifestyle I'd had all my days, one of luxury and free of worries.

Yes, I could get into that role. I'd have a jolly good time while I was in it too.

Chapter Seven

In our room, I stripped out of my clothes. Leon was doing the same behind me. I giggled, thinking it fun to have a race to see who could get naked the fastest. With thoughts of Cauli pushed firmly to the back of my mind, I vowed to enjoy what was left of the night. I had fun and frolics ahead of me with Leon, or Mr Ponsonby if I were going to be correct about it. And correct I wanted to be. But how would I play my part? I had no idea how to switch from what some people would consider a common woman into someone who was at the other end of the scale. Yet I'd gone from Mad Mandy to Pussy Pwoar without that much trouble. Yes, it had seemed weird at first to pretend to be someone else, but once I'd gotten into it I'd been on a roll.

I can do this too. Be a posh woman. How hard can it be, anyway?

I thought about all the rich people I'd seen on TV. It seemed all they did was wear nice, expensive clothes from Harrods, or wherever they got them from, and talk as though they had a plum in their mouths. Oh, and they waved their hands about a lot in expansive gestures, perhaps giving a disdainful look or two at people they deemed beneath them, as though they'd stepped in something rather squishy and smelly. And said things like spiffing and smashing. And laughed like horses neighing.

I sucked in a deep breath.

Come on, get this sexy business started. If you don't, the moment will pass.

I'd taken off all but my underwear.

"Mr Ponsonby, dear, would you mind removing my bra? One is finding it difficult to reach round and unclasp it." I was such a liar.

I was standing by the bed, near the foot, and stared into the bathroom to have something to focus on so I didn't start laughing. I'd sounded so unlike me it was hilarious. My casual clothes were something Mrs Ponsonby would never wear in a million years. Not even when she tended to her trillion or so horses and floated around her kitchen in her black silk peignoir and dainty high-heeled slippers with a puff of feathers on top. I had the fleeting image of me floating around the room but it didn't last long. I had a feeling you had to be a slim sort to pull that off and slim I most certainly wasn't.

Later, I looked forward to seeing Leon in a suit, his hair quaffed with wax like a posh man, but I had other ideas in mind before he got himself all spruced up.

"Of course," he said.

I sensed him come closer.

"Although one rather likes seeing you this way, woman. In just your underwear."

Woman. I loved the way he'd said that.

"Really," I said, trying to keep a quiver out of my voice. "And why would that be?"

"It covers all the parts one wants to see."

I frowned. That didn't make sense to me. Why would he want me covered up if he wanted to see what was covered? "All the more reason to take them off." I scrabbled inside my mind for an appropriate first name for him. And one for me. Calling him Mr Ponsonby might prove to be a mouthful after a while. "Elizabeth wants Henry to remove her garments and see what he wants to see."

"Ah, but Henry likes things left to the imagination sometimes."

"I see." At least I thought I did. I pondered what he'd said for a moment. "So you're not the type of fellow who enjoys bosoms spilling from the tops of frocks or bottoms peeking from beneath high hemlines? Don't you like to see a flash of leg through the slit in a dress? I have such a dress and I'd planned to wear it to the casino. I don't believe for one minute you wouldn't find it appealing. I suspect all heterosexual men would."

Didn't every man like that kind of thing? Wasn't that what they commented on in pubs? I'd seen Leon, Gary and Marshall ogling just that kind of thing in the past.

"At one time I rather enjoyed it."

"Yes, one was just about to say I recall a time when you three were staring at a young hussy in our drinking establishment. She was rather coarsely dressed, if I remember correctly, and she had spillage all over the place. I think one of you said 'pwoar' and the other said 'Would you get a load of that?' Of course, one found that type of behavior distinctly unseemly, but there you go."

When are you going to touch me? Come closer?

"But," he said, "it grew old quickly. Seeing that sort of thing... It gives too much away. Don't misunderstand me, one likes the swell of a breast or two as much as the next person, but every so often I find it enjoyable to wonder what's beneath such fabrics as lace and silk or, indeed, denim or leather if the lady had a mind to wear it."

Oh, he was good at this posh man thing, had the wording down to a T.

"That's delightful. Tell me, what type of underwear do you like best?"

I thought of my corset and me wearing it the first time we'd been intimate. He'd certainly seemed to like it. Was my relatively plain bra and knickers of today a comedown?

"I like any underwear you choose to put on. Whatever makes you comfortable."

"So if I decided to wear my comfortable off-white granny knickers and my sports bra that has gone frightfully ragged around the straps, you wouldn't object?" I smiled.

"I suppose I wouldn't. Whatever you wear, you look delightful to me."

God love the bones of him.

"This talk is all very well, Henry, but there's still the matter of my bra being clasped to attend to. I'm sure you wouldn't wish me to stand here getting more than a little chilly while I wait for you to do it. Good Lord, I have goosebumps you're taking so long."

"I do apologize, woman."

He was there then, right behind me, his body heat bristling the hairs on my back. I held my breath, waiting for that first touch. He managed to undo it without making contact. No brush of his fingertips on my skin. No heat from his breath on my nape. Oh, the dastardly bugger was teasing me terribly.

He snapped it open. The relief on my boobs was instant and immense. If I could get away with wearing no bra without my chest looking like two pendulums swung there, I would.

"Oh, wonderful," I said, tossing my bra away. It landed half in and half out of a little wicker bin. We hadn't used it yet, so I could only hope the cleaner had changed the liner from the previous occupant and that a sticky ball of chewing gum hadn't stuck itself to my glorious garment. "Now I need help with my knickers. I've discovered I absolutely can't get undressed by myself." I tittered a laugh. "Isn't that insane?"

"Conveniently so."

Would he try to take my knickers off without touching me too?

"But yes, your knickers will need removing. But first I'd like to say that knowing your breasts are exposed yet I still can't see them… That is quite divine."

A shiver of excitement went through me. Was he seeing my bosoms in his mind's eye? I covered them with my forearms, plumping them up so they resembled the spillage we'd mentioned earlier. Was he imagining that too?

"Dear God, Elizabeth!"

I almost swung round to see what the matter was.

"I know full well why you did that," he said.

I smiled again. "And why did I?"

"Because you know I'll be seeing those voluptuous mounds of yours in my head now."

I wanted to laugh at *mounds*. "I don't know what you're talking about." I paused. Cleared my throat. "My knickers, my good man?"

My skin warmed slightly where he was possibly holding a finger at the top of my arse. I was wearing a thong, unusual for me as I tended not to like the way they felt on my rear but they'd come as a set with the bra. The thin strip of fabric that acted as the main band didn't sit flush on my skin, leaving a gap between it and my body. He managed to tug them down without touching me at all.

I could have boiled over with frustration, yet it was incredibly sexy, having him so close. The thong slid down my legs, and I stepped out of it, flicking it away with a toe and praying it didn't cuddle up with my bra. It didn't.

"That's delightful," I said. "Now I'm naked and I have no idea what to do next."

"I'm sure you have something in mind. I can't imagine you have nothing going through that pretty little head of yours."

"What does a woman usually do when she's naked and a man is standing behind her, naked too? And I assume you *are* naked."

"That would be telling, would it not?" He breathed heavily. "And I assume a woman would want the man to touch her. After all, if she's asked him to remove her underwear, she has to trust him. Therefore, she might well want some attention. *Sexual* attention."

He was laying it on thick, playing the game well, and this side of him was so thrilling I didn't want it to end, yet conversely I wished it would hurry up. I could turn around now knowing we'd get to it straight away — I wouldn't be able to keep my hands off him — but I'd never know how it would have turned out if I'd remained facing this way.

"Gosh, you're very rude," I said. "Saucy."

"Am I indeed. I could be ruder. Saucier. But is that what you want?"

I resisted screeching that of course it was what I bloody well wanted, but that wasn't a Mrs Ponsonby response. "I would find that utterly exhilarating. Please, do carry on."

"I'm looking at your backside, the way it curves. The way, if I spread those plump cheeks of yours apart, I'd see the lower parts of your..." He inhaled deeply. Exhaled slowly. *"Cunt."*

Oh, good grief!

I swallowed my response, which would have been to tell him to stop tormenting me and to grab me, feel me, fuck me. To—

Throw me on the bed, God damn you, and ravish me.

"My cunt. Yes, you would see that—*if* you spread my plump cheeks apart."

"But I won't."

I could have sagged with disappointment.

"Do you know," he went on, "you have a beautiful set of swells there. Almost an exact match for the front, I feel."

I glanced down at my chest. Was my arse *that* big?

"I sincerely hope not," I said. "Having a bottom at the front..."

"As I said, beautiful." He didn't speak for a few seconds, then, "I brought something with me for our trip."

"Did you?" *What on earth could it be?* I racked my brains trying to work it out. Did he mean something *sexual?* Or was he going to change the subject, divert from what we were doing in order to tease me for longer? "I can't even begin to imagine."

"I'm sure you could if I gave you some clues."

"Oh, Henry Ponsonby, you're such a flirt!"

"Think back to our first night together."

Immediately, I remembered how I'd felt back then. Panicked, out of my depth. Thinking I couldn't be the woman he'd expect. That I would never measure up to his idea of what a woman should be like — or the kind of woman I'd thought he liked. I'd been so wrong. I saw us in my room, him on the chair, me prancing around in my corset.

"You brought me a corset?" I asked.

"No. Try again."

The chair, that had to be it. "You've brought one of those little compact chairs that fold away into almost nothing?"

"Why ever would I want to bring that?"

"So I could sit in it like you sat in mine?"

"No. Try again."

A whisper of air breezed over my back. Had he moved away? The sound of his suitcase being touched sounded, then his clothes being jostled. A crackle, like a paper bag. Then the *shh* of something else came next, throwing me into confusion. My knees buckled at my thought of him taking whatever he'd brought with him out of his case. The *shh* noise came again. Was he stroking it?

"Cast your mind back, Elizabeth," he said. "Listen to what I'm doing."

I couldn't think but I could listen. It was fabric, definitely fabric. Not knowing for sure was driving me mad with curiosity. Frustration threatened to set up home inside me, and I so didn't want that. The *shh* was reminiscent of a necktie being threaded through fingers. Silk on skin.

What's he holding, what's he holding...? What else makes that sound?

I closed my eyes to concentrate better. Saw my room again.

Chair. Bed. Wardrobe door ajar. My shoes, lots of shoes, all in a tumble. My lamp. The full-length mirror where he spotted who I really was. My top drawer open a bit. Bras and knickers poking out. I went through them trying to find a decent set to wear. What else? Come on, what else?

All I could recall was him on the chair, me sitting on him, him not knowing who I was because his eyes were covered with—

"A blindfold?"

He didn't answer.

"Is that what you have there?" I asked. "What kind? The sort that just covers the eyes, or a long strip of material you'd need to tie around my head? That's it, isn't it? I got it right." Silence. "Henry?"

"That is correct."

I let out a long breath. My cheeks were getting hot so I blew out again, directing the air upwards so my face would cool. I pressed my arms tighter over my chest—my nipples had perked and ached, ached, ached.

"Why did you bring it?" I whispered.

Had he liked wearing one that much? Or was he just being romantic in wanting to recreate our first time? And if he had liked it, why hadn't he said so before now? We'd done many things during our times together since that first night but a blindfold hadn't featured again.

"Because I want..." He stopped doing whatever it was he'd been doing with the blindfold. The quiet was astounding. "Because I want you to feel how I felt. I want you to know what it's like to be touched without being able to see. I want you to touch me without the aid of sight. I want, my dear lady, to give back to you what you gave to me."

Chapter Eight

I snapped my eyes open. Blinked away the dampness there. He was so thoughtful, so bloody wonderful.

"What do you think to that?" he asked. "Is it something you would like to try?"

"Yes. That would be lovely. And oh, Mr Ponsonby, that's... That's so very dear of you to want to return the gesture." My voice had sounded rough and had the quality of an emotional woman clinging to it, ivy to brick, barnacles to hulls. I hoped I could shake it off. I couldn't break down now with the sniffles. That wouldn't be becoming. A lady such as I was supposed to have a stiff upper lip, as rigid as...something rigid, and to lower myself to histrionics was simply not allowed.

I composed myself, straightening my shoulders and lowering my arms to my sides.

"Then I'll put it on you, shall I?" he asked.

"If you wouldn't mind."

We'd done well to stay in role, when all I wanted was to turn around and fling myself at him. To kiss his face a hundred times and tell him I loved, loved, loved him. I remained in place, though, anticipating him putting the blindfold on. Many seconds passed, maybe even a minute, with me chanting *hurry up* inside my head and thinking he'd begin, then when he didn't, going through the chant all over again.

A soft touch of fabric slithered over my shoulder. Black. Satin. The ends decorated with tassels. It could have passed as Mrs Ponsonby's regular scarf, one she wore tied tightly at the neck along with a little black dress and sophisticated high heels while at a cocktail party. Or perhaps it would go well with her riding gear, flapping out behind her as she raced on her stallion, beige jodhpurs, a black velvet hunting jacket and leather boots completing her ensemble.

The scarf was cold despite him having held it and I shivered. I lifted one hand to touch it, rubbing it between fingers and thumb. It slid in my grasp.

"What's it like?" he asked.

"Delicate." It was also wide — wide enough that when bunched around my eyes it would still span quite a bit of my face. I wouldn't be able to see below it. And the darkness would be absolute, I was sure of it.

I let it go.

His forearms appeared beside my face, one hand holding the scarf, and he also took hold of another part with his free hand. He held the material up in front of me so a long rectangle of it blocked out my view of the bathroom and the remainder dangled either side. It bore fold marks, several of them that made squares.

He began scrunching it into a narrower band. "You'll look so pretty in this. So pretty..."

And I'd never see it. Never know what that black strip would look like over my face. Part of me wanted to — I had the need to see what he would see — but the only way to do that was by me peeking once it was on or him taking a picture.

A picture? Would you let him do that? Take one? Of you with no clothes on?

I would.

"Use my phone and take a picture of my face when I have it on?" I asked. "But make sure you turn it back off quickly. I don't want anyone bothering us."

"Christ…" He'd slipped back into being Leon. "I mean, as you wish, Elizabeth."

He moved the blindfold toward me until it was only an inch or so away. It smelled new, indeed fresh from the packet. He touched it to my face, erasing most of the light, and I stared at it, seeing nothing but blackness ahead. The tassels tickled my shoulders as he dragged them over my shoulders, then the ends kissed my back. I assumed they were swinging.

I closed my eyes.

"This should be comfortable when I tie it," he said, securing it at the side of my head, still managing not to touch me in any way. "If it's too tight, please say."

"It's fine." The pressure it created on my face was strange at first, a pushing force that made it seem as though my cheeks bulged out of the bottom. On my forehead it felt tighter, steely though not uncomfortable in the slightest — the same over my nose. In my head I could see myself in it and got a kick of excitement from the visual.

Have you got that kick, Henry? Is it making you hard?

He must have let the scarf go — the material pooled on my shoulder then slid to rest over my collarbone. It warmed quickly. I reached up again to stroke it, to feel it on my face, dancing my fingertips across the satin.

My nipples grew harder, straining as if asking to be handled.

"The photo," he said. "One moment."

I heard the scrape of my phone as he took it from the dressing table. The noise it made when he swiped the screen into life. The click of him accessing the camera function. I held myself still. Waited.

The camera made a whir.

It was done.

"Tell me what you're feeling, Elizabeth."

"Asking myself if I'm mad to have let you take the picture. Safe—but I didn't think I would. Sexy. Excited."

"Good. We can erase the image if you'd prefer. After you've seen it."

"We'll see."

Silence.

Then, "Take three steps backwards."

I did so.

"Now one step to your left, then again until your leg meets with the bed."

I obeyed, the coolness of the overhanging quilt pressing into my calf.

"Now imagine you're standing at quarter past on the clock. Turn to half past."

I took a moment to think it over—I hadn't been expecting to have to work out a mathematical problem. I turned, the backs of both legs pressing against the bed.

"Now sit."

Despite knowing the bed was right there behind me, I was a little unnerved. I bent my knees and lowered my hands slowly until my fingertips met with the duvet. I pushed my hands flat to it then sat.

"That's it, my lady. Now fall onto your back."

I swallowed down a pinch of what I assumed was natural mistrust. I trusted him, I honestly did, but to have one of my senses taken away was as unsettling as it was exhilarating.

I fell back. The bed was there, as I'd known it would be, but still I breathed out a sigh of relief. I spread my fingers then clutched the bedding — perhaps silly but it was something…security while I was vulnerable.

"And now I see what your underwear had hidden," he said. "What you had hidden by facing away from me. It's all there, exposed, for me to look at. What a delight. The wait, the not seeing, was worth it. I wish you could see what I see, *how* I see it."

I resisted letting the quilt go and covering myself. He'd taught me — and I'd taught myself over the past months — that I shouldn't be ashamed of my body. The old insecurities still lingered, though, and I suspected they always would, but they weren't as sharp and spiteful as they had been. I breathed steadily, coaching myself to remain in control, but the lack of sight was affecting me more than I'd imagined it would.

"This is…strange," I said. "I want to see you so badly. Is that because I can't?"

"If you're feeling anything like I did, it drove me mad. I wanted to rip the blindfold off, but a certain woman told me that wasn't allowed. Then when I did… Seeing you was like staring at the best thing, the most beautiful thing."

Damn him. My eyes were leaking.

"You say such nice things, Mr Ponsonby."

"You deserve them to be said."

I didn't think I could manage an answer.

"I brought something else with me," he said. "Would you like me to get it?"

"Yes."

"You might not want me to use it, although… Yes, on second thought I think you might. I did notice one time while in your bedroom that you have something like it."

He wasn't the type to nose about, so whatever it was he must have seen it lying around. It had to be something rude, didn't it?

"I'm sure if I have something the same it'll be fine, Henry."

I gripped the bedding tighter while listening to his soft footsteps as he moved away. I thought about any toys I had in my room and came up with a set of handcuffs. That would tally with the blindfold and what he'd done so far tonight—the not touching. Maybe he wanted me to have two senses taken away.

More sounds of him at his suitcase. Another crackle of a paper bag. The snap of plastic casing being popped open? The slide of something being removed. His footsteps as he returned. A shiver of his breathing.

The build-up was excruciating. If I could see I realized it wouldn't be so stimulating, but my God I *wanted* to see. It seemed every nerve on my body was on edge, buzzing, urging all my hairs to stand on end. I breathed shallow, bubbles of tense excitement thrumming in my chest, and told myself to keep calm, to not want everything so damn quickly. I had to admit I hadn't felt this way before. Every bit of me was alive, on high alert, me tense as if waiting for something to pounce. Yet he wouldn't pounce, not tonight. It was clear he wanted to draw this out.

Something cold and weighty was placed on the soft pad at the top of my cunt. I inhaled sharply, my mind scrambling with possibilities. It wasn't handcuffs—too heavy, too thick—and it didn't give me the feeling it was a paddle or a whip. I didn't own either of those so...

"A vibrator, Henry?"

"And if it is?"

"Switch it on."

"Not just yet."

"Oh, God..." This was pleasurable torture but torture all the same.

"I want to describe it to you. It's small—smaller than yours. Like a bullet but bigger. It's black. Shiny. And there are two flat flaps at the end. Do you know what they are, Elizabeth?"

I had an idea. "So it doesn't slip right up my bottom?"

He dragged it down my cunt. "So it doesn't slip right up your bottom. Open your legs. Wide. That's it. Now lift your legs—put your feet at the edge of the bed. Good."

I was so exposed, so open, and wanted to see his expression as he looked at me. He lowered the vibrator to my rear hole, pushing a little. The skin was tight, resisting, so the bullet tip seemed to bounce on it.

"How is that, Elizabeth?"

"Odd but nice. It's a dull feeling. Heavy."

He took it away. "It might be cold in a moment."

Immediately, I knew what he was going to do. I could say no, could protest, but I didn't want to. He took maybe a minute then came back. And so did the pressure on my arse, except this time it was very cold and wet. I gasped from the shock of it. He pushed slowly, and I bit my bottom lip as he eased the bullet into my backside. Suddenly it slid right in, quickly, and one of the flaps he'd mentioned pressed into the strip of skin between my entrances, the other below my pucker. I felt fuller than I did when he had his cock in my cunt, the muscles tighter, clenching around the bullet in a forceful grip. The skin of my opening was stretched around it, taut, an alien sensation but not unpleasant.

"How is that?" he asked.

"It's good. I'm just...just getting used to it. I need a second..."

I breathed in then out, in then out, my heart pulsing hard. I relaxed my grip on the duvet, flexed my hands into star shapes to stop myself grabbing it again.

Then he switched the bullet on.

I jerked my hips upwards, arse leaving the bed, and let out a startled cry. My whole midsection erupted with life, streaks of sensation flickering through my veins, over my skin. I lowered my arse and groaned — the buzz was sending echoic waves up my folds and into my clit.

"Oh, this is... Oh!" I clamped my lips together.

Then the mattress dipped and he was over me, his presence right *there*, the feel of him, although he wasn't touching, so very near. And at last, he lowered onto me, his skin seeming blazing hot. I wrapped my arms around his back, pulling him closer, reveling in our closeness. He thrust his cock into my cunt, and oh, his thickness combined with the bullet stretched me to capacity. I couldn't breathe for several heartbeats, opened my eyes from the shock of his entry even though I still couldn't see, and dragged my nails down his back, wanting to score how it felt into him.

He fucked me hard and fast, such a contrast to how slow he'd been up until now, and I pushed up, lifting my arse off the bed, needing him inside me as far as he could go.

"I feel it," he said. "It's fucking fine on my cock."

Gone was Mr Ponsonby. Leon had returned, my man with the rough words.

"On my fucking cock," he said again, riding me harder, faster.

I clamped onto his arse, letting him take me wherever he would. He raised off my chest, must have propped himself up on both hands. His mouth covered my nipple and he sucked, tugged, sucked, dragging a loud groan out of me that turned into a keen as my orgasm hit. It was all-consuming, sending my mind spinning, my senses into somersaults. I couldn't think of anything except coming, whoosh after whoosh of undulating pleasure that rippled so violently I almost screamed. The intensity was insane and just kept going, no let-up, crashing into me time and again. He came, jerking stiffly, with a shout of satisfaction. I shook my head from side to side, trying to get the blindfold off, wanting to see him. He wrenched it away, stared down at me as he thrust on, then bent his head to kiss me fast and with passion. I held on, thinking if I let him go I'd fall — somewhere I wouldn't be able to get back from. My arse was going numb but my cunt was alive with aftershocks, the type I'd feel long after we were done.

He slowed then rolled us so I was on top of him. He reached down and switched the bullet off then pulled it out nice and slow. It thudded to the bed. We panted, staring at one another, me amazed that an orgasm could be so electrifying.

"I take it you enjoyed that, Mrs Ponsonby."

"Oh, God, yes." I struggled to get my breathing back to normal. "God, yes."

"Now look at this." He reached across the bed for my phone.

I blushed, already embarrassed at what I would see. He brought the picture up and I closed my eyes, asking myself if I really wanted to look at it.

"It's lovely," he said. "Please look."

I opened my eyes. Saw a stranger on the screen. She seemed so sexy, so not me. Yet it was me, no one else. She was sultry, waiting to be fucked, wanting to be fucked and touched and kissed and...

"Oh!" I said.

"Do you see what I see now, when I look at you?" he asked.

"Yes," I whispered. And I really thought I did.

Chapter Nine

The night had it in mind to freeze my bare skin off, I would have put a bet on it. The slit in my dress gaped open as I walked from our hotel. I was perhaps colder than I would normally have been, owing to me having had a shower just before we'd left. My teeth chattered, and Leon did his best to keep me warm by hugging me tight to his side.

"Please, put on my jacket," he said.

"No, it's one minute away, don't be silly."

We entered the casino seconds later. It was unlike anything I'd ever visited before. If I'd thought it would be like those little rooms on the seafront where people gathered to excitedly play coin push machines I'd have been wrong. I didn't know *what* I'd expected, really, but this place definitely hadn't been it. It was glamorous — so much so that even with my posh dress and fancy hairstyle I felt like I didn't fit in.

Come on, you've been through this as Pussy. Let Mrs Ponsonby take over completely.

The lower half of the walls were wooden, their carved square inserts varnished to a high sheen. They reflected all who stood near them. The top half was wallpaper, burgundy with gold stripes, which gave off a rich feel. The large windows were made with mottled glass, and deep red drapes hung from golden rails. The windows were so high that long, thin ropes dangled from the ends of the poles in order for the curtains to be closed.

Everywhere screamed rich and elegant, something I wasn't.

You can do this. No one here knows you haven't got a pot to piss in.

I took a deep breath, ready to heed my own advice. I glanced around as though I'd been in a casino a thousand times before and knew what I was doing. Lights flashed from the slot machines on the right-hand wall, a cacophony of jingles coming out of them as well as the tinkle of coins falling into the payout troughs. People were seated in front of them on tall stools, feeding in coin after coin, their body language that of expectation and the hope that they'd hit the jackpot. I remembered feeling like that as a child when we'd holidayed at Hayling Island. I'd been mesmerized by the flickering lights and the thought that my ten pence might magically turn into a pound if I hit the right combination.

I never had.

In front of us were the gaming tables, so many of them that I lost count after about ten. Men in suits surrounded them, as well as women in far grander dresses than mine—real Mrs Ponsonbys and more than a few Miss Richness and Madam Spendalots. A different world but one I wanted to fit into, if only for the next couple of hours. Laughter tittered, throats were cleared. Croupiers—young sexy ladies dressed in the same slim-fitting black dresses—doled out cards. Security men flanked not only the edges of the vast room but hovered near tables too. Chips tapped against each other, chatter came off as a big hum of dull melodies, and the occasional whoop from a winner rent the air.

"Bloody hell," I said, leaning into Mr Ponsonby. "How the other half live."

"But we're the other half now," he said. "That's what you told me before we came in. We have to *be* them, act just like them. So" — he parked his hand at the small of my back and guided me forward — "what would you like to do first, m'lady?"

"The slots," I said. "I'm not risking any of my wages on those gaming tables. I don't even know how to play anyway."

"But of course you do, being Mrs Ponsonby. What you meant to say was you didn't fancy playing the tables tonight, good sir."

He was getting right into it and I was ridiculously pleased.

"Yes, you're quite right, darling." I nodded at the slots. "Lead on, dear fellow."

He guided us through the throng of people who stood about watching the games in play. Those gathered here even smelled different. More luxurious. I'd bet some of the women's perfume cost as much as my weekly wage.

What must it be like to buy something so expensive and not think anything of it?

I'd winced in the past at buying scent at thirty pounds a pop — *and* I'd felt it had been too much. How the other half lived indeed.

Two slots were empty, side by side, and we perched on the stools. My dress slid to the side, showing off my thigh, and instead of hiding it I left it on display. It felt daring and so liberating that I held off a giggle.

"I'll just go and get us some change," Mr Ponsonby said. "Won't be a minute."

While he was gone I watched a woman on the machine beside me. She was clearly an expert, peering up at what was coming next on the reels. She wore a velvet gown, more fitting for going to some ball or other, I thought, and little velvet shoes to match. She held a cup full of coins in one hand while poising her finger over the start button with the other. She pressed it, held her breath and widened her eyes. The machine warbled a manic little tune then a few pence slid into the winning gulley. She squealed then inspected the reels again.

I turned to stare at the slot machine in front of me, not having a clue how to play the game. There were vague directions in gaudy colored boxes on the machine front but nothing that gave totally clear instruction. It looked as though I had to match cherries and lemons to get a low win, but the jackpot was reserved for three strawberries and the prize was two hundred pounds. I'd wet myself if I won it. Excitement bubbled in my tummy, and I glanced around to catch sight of whether Mr Ponsonby was on his way back.

He stood in a queue outside a booth, three people in front of him, and turned to see me looking. I waved, wanting to bounce on my stool, so ready to play the machine I could hardly stand it. He waved back, blew me a kiss and straightened himself to his full height. I imagined he'd slipped out of role and was mentally putting himself back in it. I did the same, adopting a more ladylike pose from the slouch I had been in.

A group of men, all with majorly bushy beards and moustaches, walked toward the queue from the far end of the casino. They were deep in conversation, their heads bent, and I wondered whether they were here for a team-building exercise with work or on a night out after closing a business deal. The possibilities as to why they were here were endless, and I stared in fascination as they rounded Mr Ponsonby and continued toward me. The woman beside me got up, as did the old lady next to her, and the men came to stand in the spaces they'd created. I faced my machine so they didn't think I was listening, putting my handbag on my lap so I could root through my purse to see if I had any change I could use while I waited for the love of my life to join me.

"Table two," one of them said. "Right by the door. See it through those two machines there?" A pause, then, "Hit it and hit it hard. There's a fuck load of chips on it, enough to cash in at their other branch in London. Get them and get out. We'll be outside as planned."

My stomach rolled over. What the hell was going on in my life? First a bank robbery, then the jewelry theft, and now a casino hit? Or had I imagined it, hearing what he'd said?

I had the urge to get up but remained still, not wanting to draw attention to myself. I found some coins and drew them out of my purse, hand shaking as I lifted it to pop some money in the slot. I dropped it, let out a stupid little yelp of surprise, and slid off the stool to pick it up off the floor. While down there, I pretended I couldn't find it, wanting to be as small as possible, hoping they'd see me as some silly woman who didn't know her arse from her elbow so wouldn't possibly have got any idea as to what they were up to.

"It's there," one of them said, his voice an all too familiar rasp.

Oh, God, it's bloody Cauli...

My chest tightened and I found it a struggle to breathe. I couldn't stand up, couldn't let him see me, so remained crouched. One of them toed the coin toward me and I lifted it, mumbling thank you in a voice that didn't belong to me but our dear queen. My pulse thudded in my ears — so loud, so *there* — and I realized I couldn't stay down even if I wanted to. They'd wonder why I didn't get up.

I stood, careful to keep my face from being seen, then sat on the stool. I fed the coin into the slot, successfully this time, and jabbed at the red flashing start button. The reels spun, a whizz of strawberries, lemons and cherries, and a blare of music erupted, making me jump.

Don't come back yet, Leon. Just stay where you are.

I wanted to glance to my right to see him but didn't dare. The men were still there.

"So, give it five minutes after we've left, all right? Then make out you're joining the game. Might take you a while to get a seat because it's a full table at the minute. Remember, it takes as long as it takes, got it? If you rush to join in it'll look suspicious. And don't forget, the guard by the table and the other by the door won't stop you leaving. There'll just happen to be a convenient commotion they need to attend to."

The reels stopped one after the other. Lemon, cherry, strawberry. I popped another coin in and played again.

"Time to get this shit started," he said.

Please, just go away...

In my peripheral I saw the men start to walk off. All except one, who leaned close to my ear. I froze, staring at the reels as though my life depended on it.

"And you," he said. "There you are again. What are you, a fucking copper?"

"I have no idea what you're talking about," I said in Mrs Ponsonby's voice, gazing ahead at the flashing lights. "No idea at all. Run along now." *Why the hell did I say that?* "As I said, no idea what you're talking about."

"Best you keep it that way an' all. And like *I* said earlier, if I see you again... Just so happens that me causing a scene in here with you now isn't to my liking. You got away lightly — this time. But I fucking mean it, if you're anywhere near me again, I'll bloody have you. And that bloke of yours."

I went cold, my skin clammy. I shook all over, unable to control it, and battled with being sick. He moved away, and as he'd been the one issuing instructions, I knew he'd be outside somewhere, waiting for one of the others to do the hit. When Leon and I left, they'd be there, watching. Our hotel was only two buildings along. He'd spot us. Know where we were staying.

And those beards they were wearing. Fake and so creepy.

Oh, fucking hell. Shit, shit, shit...

Then he was gone, as though he'd never been there at all. Had never said those horrible things in my ear. My life had suddenly turned into a mad movie, one I didn't want to star in. I turned, so bloody relieved to see Leon heading for me.

He stopped by my side and touched my shoulder. "What was that all about?"

"I shouldn't say, not here. We need to, um, move. Find somewhere private."

"What the hell?" He glanced around, obviously in search of the men.

"Don't," I said, lifting my hand to cover his. "Honestly, you do *not* want to go and find them."

"I do if they've upset you."

"No." I got off the stool, stood on tiptoes and gave the performance of my life. I hugged him with my arms around his neck, pressing my cheek to his. "It was Cauli. And they're going to rob this bloody place!"

"Fuck me," he said, holding me tight. "What, did you hear them discussing it or something?"

"Yes, right by me, and it's no good telling the security guards because two of them are in on it. Who knows if more are? And if we use my mobile to ring the police or go back to the hotel to do it—Cauli is going to be outside, he said so, watching. He'll see us go in. You never know with these types. What if he belongs to a massive gang who have loads of people in it and he tells them he saw us and, and, and they follow us back home and—"

"Stop it," he said, easing back so he could look at me. He held my face in both hands. "We'll sort this. Leave through a back door and go into our hotel the same way."

"But we'll get stopped. It'll look dodgy."

"Not if I have anything to do with it."

He let my face go then took my hand. Leading me to the money booth, where no one was queuing, he smiled at the woman inside it. "This is probably an unusual request, but I wonder if you can help me."

"I'll try to, sir."

"My girlfriend's ex is outside—bit of a tricky situation as you can imagine—and she doesn't want to see him, or for him to see her. He always starts trouble, you see, so I was wondering, is there any chance we can be let out the back? Our hotel's only two doors down—is there an alley behind here or something we could use?"

She smiled. "It's an unusual request, but I don't see a problem. Hang on while I call security so they can help you."

"Thank you," Leon said.

She spoke quietly into a phone then a guard appeared seconds later. He looked us up and down, must have decided we weren't up to anything, then led us to a rear fire exit. Leon took his jacket off and draped it over my shoulders. This time I didn't protest. The guard opened the door, and we went out into an extremely cold yard that was fenced in. Goosebumps popped up on my arms despite the jacket. Leon rubbed them through the material and once again I was so grateful to have him. No one had ever cared about me like this.

I glanced about, wondering if Cauli had a man out here keeping watch. Tall refuse bins stood to the left, one with its lid partially open where rubbish had been piled high. Light from inside the casino spilled out from the still open door over two cars that were parked ahead, a Mercedes and a Jaguar. The security man walked between them then strode across the yard to open a gate using a set of keys that clinked loudly. We followed.

"Thanks," Leon said as we went out into an alley. "Really appreciate this."

The guard didn't respond. He stared for a moment, a street light down the way making him seem sinister and out to cause a bit of menace. I couldn't look away then told myself that he'd have to look threatening, considering the job he had. If people had him near their table they'd think twice before cheating. I knew I bloody would. He sniffed then closed the gate. I had the mad idea he'd memorized our faces, and even if he wasn't involved with Cauli's gang he may well have glared at us like that anyway. It was a fact casinos got robbed—he could have thought we were some kind of diversion tactic before the main thieving event.

"Come on," I said, feeling watched even though he'd gone. "Let's get the hell away from here."

I tottered along in my heels, dodging litter and a pile of dog's shit. The path was made of uneven bricks— that didn't help me walk faster—and I looked at the backs of the buildings, so thankful to see our hotel's rear façade matched the front. The sky-blue paint looked muddy in the scant light. Turning into Smithin Lodge's yard, which was smaller than that of the casino, I let out a long breath and looked around. It was much the same as the casino's except everything was squashed into a smaller space and there weren't any cars. The refuse bins were larger, though.

Big enough for someone to hide in.

I stayed glued to Leon's side and spotted another gate and fence ahead. I pushed the gate open, realizing the yard had been sectioned into two parts, thankful to be greeted with a garden used by the smoking clientele. Plastic chairs and tables dotted a patio, all set beneath a white marquee. Large French doors showed a sitting room of sorts behind them, and we went inside, my legs wobbly from the encounter with Cauli. It seemed by silent communication we'd opted to stay quiet. While we waited for a lift in the foyer, I didn't glance out of the front window or even face it in case Cauli happened to be there and spotted us. Then again, with my bright red dress, I'd stand out anyway.

Shit.

We made it to our room without incident. Once inside, the door locked, I scrabbled in my bag for my phone.

"We need to ring the police," I said. "Tell them what I heard."

Leon was at the window, peering outside through a crack in the curtains. "There's definitely something going on."

"What do you mean?"

I walked to the window, crouching so Leon could still look out. A car was parked on the opposite side of the road, big, black, its windows tinted, the headlights off. It stood out sitting there between a Mini and some other small car, but it might have only seemed that way because of what I knew. Yes, that would be the type of car they'd need to collect the thief, something to roar off in, the occupants shielded from view by those dark windows.

"Use the hotel phone," he said. "You might be on there for quite a while if they take what you say seriously. You don't want your battery running out."

I went to the bedside cabinet and picked up the phone, dialed and waited for the emergency services dispatcher to go through the usual patter. I gabbled out what I'd heard in the casino, and she asked me to repeat myself several times.

"I don't know when," I said, "just that it's tonight at some point. The man said they had to wait for a convenient moment, but there's a bloody big SUV parked out the front of our hotel and they could be in it. He threatened me—he did it earlier on too, at the Pleasure Beach when he robbed that woman's jewelry and—"

"One moment." The line went quiet, then, "I'm transferring you to someone. Please stay on the line."

I moved back to the window, going down on my knees to look out. The SUV was still there. Leon stroked the top of my head, and I covered the mouthpiece.

"I know I like pretending to be other people, but this is bloody ridiculous," I said.

"Well, it's livened up the night. Who knew you'd be a covert spy when you went for your holiday in Blackpool?"

"I'd rather not be, thank you. I was doing fine as Mrs Ponsonby until Cauli turned up."

"Hello?" a man said.

I jumped and took my hand from the mouthpiece. "Hello?"

"I'm Detective Broadley. Would you mind telling me what happened?"

Chapter Ten

Detective Broadley seemed to fill the doorway. He had a full beard, greying in places, which joined his sideburns to create the visual that if he had the notion to pull his hair, everything would come off in one piece, leaving him looking like a boiled egg. In my mind's eye I saw him bald and stopped myself before I let out a nervous giggle. Now was not the time to entertain my mad imagination. I stepped back to let him in, refusing to think of other men with other, more sinister beards. He entered, stood by the door, folded his hands over his ample belly and rocked on his heels. Was that a requirement of being a detective? They did the same thing on TV too.

You watch far too much TV, Mandy.

"I appreciate you doing this," he said, fluttering his fingers like he played piano.

I was glad he *did* appreciate it. I'd been a mass of nerves before he'd arrived, convinced that Cauli would know I'd had something to do with the police foiling their robbery when they converged on them after the heist.

"That's okay," I said, closing the door. It wasn't okay, though. None of this was. "But as you can appreciate, I'm scared. He knows my face."

"So you said on the phone." He cleared his throat. Stared at me a little too hard. "Bit of an unfortunate time for you, I'd say, seeing him in your home city then again here—and not just in the casino but the Pleasure Beach too." He narrowed his eyes and seemed to be fighting off an expression of disbelief.

Did he think we had something to do with this? Was that why he was staring at me like that? I didn't like that idea and wanted to say so but didn't.

"It was just bad luck, us seeing him again, or even at all," I said. "It isn't something I wanted to happen. It's not like I go about wishing nutty people would cross my path. It just so happens they did. We're just regular people, aren't we, Leon, preferring to mind our own business, but it seems fate has other ideas, if such a thing exists. And if it does, it isn't very nice, is it, playing with people like this, causing trouble and worry and making me want to shit—" I needed to stop waffling. "I just want it over so we can get on with our holiday."

"I imagine you do," he said, playing a particularly fast tune on his air keyboard.

I wondered if it was *Chopsticks* at high speed.

What a strange man. Is everything destined to be weird from now on?

"Now then." He strode over to the window and looked out, hidden to anyone outside by using the curtain as cover. "There's nothing to worry about. Officers are in place, and although we don't usually involve the public like this, me being in your room and whatnot, in this instance I thought it might calm you to know you have someone here when they get caught. After all, you were rather distraught on the telephone and we like to do our duty, helping the public as much as we can."

That was nice of him to say that, but again I couldn't help but think he was harboring the idea we were a part of it. It wouldn't stop nagging at me. I had to say something.

"He was horrible last night. At the pub. I didn't know him from Adam, and he pinched my bum! And him following me to the toilet! Well, he's obviously used to getting his own way, trying to get me to... Ugh. As I said, it was horrible."

"A visiting rugby team, you said." Detective Broadley glanced at me, stared for several seconds, then turned back to the window.

"We thought they were with the rugby teams," Leon said. "Thinking about it now, they might not have been. There'd been a local match, and because some of our usual players were in the pub, we assumed... Well, you can see how it was."

"Mmm. And you'd know him again if you saw him?" the detective asked.

"God, yes," I said, going into an involuntary convulsion as an image of Cauli bombarded my mind. I wrapped my arms around my middle to stop myself looking like a drunken body-popper and gave what I imagined looked like a lame smile at my antics. "He's got one hell of a mad set of eyes on him. And funny ears. Like cauliflower or the heads of broccoli. You know, that bobbly stuff. That must have been why I thought he played rugby, but then again he could be a boxer, because they get weird ears, don't they, from being bashed or whatever. Or maybe he's just some man who gets into a lot of fights, and now I know he robbed a bank it stands to reason he would fight." I stopped myself from going further. I didn't want to go on and on, letting nerves do my speaking for me.

"Very true," Detective Broadley said. "Hey up, here we go." He wrenched the curtain across and pressed his nose to the glass.

My stomach lurched and I bolted to the window, wanting to look yet at the same time wishing I could stay out of this. Leon joined me, holding me to his side. A bearded man ran from the casino, across the road toward the SUV, a bulging bag bouncing against his arse. Someone shouted, but it was indistinct from where we stood. Police officers appeared from nowhere, ants swarming on a sweet treat. He was brought down in the middle of the road, and the SUV was surrounded within seconds. The car moved, headlights going on full beam and rudely lighting the rear of the Mini. Shouts from below filtered up, adding to the tension already at snapping point inside me. I gripped Leon's hand, squeezed tight, and wished my heart wouldn't pound quite so bloody fast.

Officers ripped open the SUV's doors, dragging the occupants onto the pavement. Pressed against the vehicle, the thiefish bastards yelled and struggled as they were cuffed. One of them looked up, seemingly right at me, and my knees weakened.

Cauli.

"That's him," I said, voice cracking. I edged away from the window, taking Leon with me. "That's the man who threatened me."

"Good that you recognized him," Detective Broadley said. "Always a bonus, that."

Nothing about this was a bonus.

"He was staring at me just then," I said. "What if he saw me, really saw me, and knows it was me?"

"This is a big hotel," Detective Broadley said. "It might have appeared that he was looking at you, but from where I'm standing it seems he's looking higher." He snatched a mobile phone from his pocket and jabbed in a few numbers. "Excuse me a moment—and please, remain in this room."

He left, closing the door behind him. I stared at Leon, a huge lump in my throat and the need to run rampaging through me. If Cauli had been looking higher, did that mean they had someone from their gang in this hotel that he needed to get the attention of? My mind spun with the possibilities.

"We can't stay here," I said, gripping Leon's lapels. "We need to leave. Go somewhere else. Go home, whatever, just get the hell out."

"We will," he said. "Once the police have finished, we will."

"And it won't be over." I left his side to pace at the foot of the bed. "We'll be asked to do one of those identity parade thingies. And a trial. What if they ask us to give evidence? What if we have to stand in the dock and Cauli's there, staring across at us? We'll have to swear on the Bible and all sorts, and I won't be able to lie then—I'll have to tell the judge it was him. And they'll ask if the accused man is in the court, and I'll have to point at him and say that yes, yes he is. What if it's like I said and Cauli has nasty people all over the place, ready to sort out people like us?"

Leon took hold of me and stopped my pacing by drawing me to him. "Stop it. They've been caught. I'm sure they'll allow us to do a video link in court. And I watched something on TV the other week. They don't do identity parades like they used to. You pick them out of a video line-up. So don't worry, okay?"

I nodded, but of course I'd worry. Wouldn't anyone?

A knock on the door startled a pathetic whimper out of me. Leon went to answer it. I stayed where I was, seemingly stuck in place by fear that it wouldn't be Detective Broadley but some nutcase who had found out what we'd done and had come to dish out their form of justice.

Detective Broadley motioned with his head for Leon to go out into the corridor. My stomach contracted at my thoughts that something had gone wrong. Were we in danger? I sank onto the bed, my mind going crazy with potential scenarios. Unable to settle, I went back to the window, keeping behind the curtain and looking out onto the road. The captured men were gone, but several people were out there, the lure of getting fodder for gossip proving too much, I suspected.

The door opened. I jumped, a barrel of nerves, and swiveled to face the door. Leon was there, minus the detective, and he closed the door behind him.

"We need to go to the station tomorrow and give a statement," he said. "And as for the identity parade, it's like I said. All done through video. We'll have to go to our station at home and see if we can pick them out once they've filmed the line-up. I'll remember Cauli or whatever it is you call him, but as for the others... Fuck knows."

He came to the window, pulled me back against him and crossed his hands over my middle. I relaxed a bit, tension going out of my shoulders, but didn't think I'd sleep well at all. I just wanted to go home, get away from here. Our holiday had been ruined.

"Do you need to pretend to be someone else?" he whispered.

"I wish I was at the moment."

"It'll be all right, you know."

"I hope so."

We stood for a long time, watching out of that window. Eventually, the police left, as did the onlookers, and the street went back to how I assumed it always was. Revelers leaving pubs sang, their rowdy songs out of tune and so like home it made me want to ring Jen or my mum. It was all very well having the police know what was going on, but what if something happened where even the police couldn't find us? We could be kidnapped or something, and no one would know until we didn't arrive back home. Outside gave me a sense of normality, though, calmed me down again. Life went on after such events, I knew that, and time would hopefully fade what had happened and I'd look back on it without being scared. But now, right now? I wanted to crawl under the duvet and never come out.

Tired, I sighed and turned in Leon's arms, pressing myself into his body and closing my eyes. "I need sleep but I don't think I'll manage it."

"You will. And I'm here. I'll stay awake with you all night if you want me to. We can try to remember other people we've seen since we got here. Play 'What's her Secret?', if you like?"

I smiled and broke away from him, going to my suitcase and rummaging about for a nightshirt. I pulled one out then went to the bathroom, stopping by the door and leaning on the jamb. "I'm so glad you're here. That this happened when I was with you. If it had been me and Jen... I'd have been more afraid."

He walked over to me, stroked the backs of his fingers down my cheek. "I'll look after you always, you know that. Whenever you're scared, happy, sad, whatever, I'll be here."

A lump came to my throat then, harsh and expanding, but I didn't want to give myself the luxury of tears. I needed to be strong, to show myself I could be, even if there was a big opportunity here to be the vulnerable one and let my man take care of me. Him wiping the tears instead of a tissue. His arms around me instead of my own. Him telling me everything would be all right instead of me whispering it to myself.

I stared into his eyes. Life was going to be so very different now. It wouldn't be me alone but us together. I'd never have to sort out any troubles by myself, working through them in my mind. I could talk them through, get his opinion, find solutions in half the time. I'd known for so long he was the man for me, and if it hadn't been for Marshall covering Leon's head with his T-shirt that time, who knew how long it would have been before we'd gotten together—if at all.

"I'll just have a shower," I said. "I feel dirty."

"I'll jump in after," he said, going to sit on the bed.

Men from my past would have insisted that they join me, fucked the fright out of me while we were in there, any excuse to get their end away. Leon was so different. He knew when to back off and when to come close.

I adored him for that.

I turned, pushed the door to, then set the water going. Stripping out of my dress, I let it fall to the tiles. I never wanted to wear it again, or be Mrs Ponsonby, even if I *did* have a brilliant time as her before we'd gone to the casino. I smiled at the memory. That was a recollection I'd take back home with me. Us, like that. Not what happened after or before.

The water was a balm to my soul. I stood beneath it while it worked its magic then washed the crime off me, the feeling of being polluted by what those men had done, what Cauli's threat had done.

Out and dried, my nightshirt enveloping me with the scent of home, I returned to the bedroom. Leon stood, stroked my cheek again as he passed, then went into the bathroom. I climbed into bed, wishing it were mine and that the mattress wasn't so hard, the pillow so fluffy. In the darkness, I waited for Leon, and when he appeared I almost allowed myself to cry. How lovely it was going to be to share my life with him. To have him around when things got tough and I needed a shoulder to cry on, someone to share my worries with. Someone to just be there and hold me, not having to say a word because sometimes words weren't needed.

He got in beside me, took me in his arms. I snuggled next to him on my side, one leg thrown over both of his, my cheek to his chest, his heartbeat thudding in my ear.

"So," he said. "That woman in the money booth. What's her secret?"

"Oh, that's easy." I smiled. "She has to work nights because she has children and they're too young to go to school in the day. She stays home to watch them, and when her husband comes in from work, she goes out. They only see each other properly at weekends, but when they do they cherish the hours. The weeks seem to go on forever for her, the weekends too fast, and she can't wait for the time when they can be with one another for longer."

"You're a soppy bugger, aren't you," he said.

"I can be."

"What else?"

I thought about it for a moment. Imagined her stuck in that booth. "She's trying to get another job, maybe one she can do from home. She sits in her booth doling out coins for notes, and all the while she's thinking of what he's doing. Putting the children in the bath then tucking them in bed. Reading them a story until they nod off. Watching TV all by himself. Falling asleep on the sofa while he waits for her to come home. She wishes she could be with him instead of where she is now."

"I'd feel the same as her," Leon said. "I did before we came away. Counted down the hours. Thought of what you were doing. If I had lunch, I'd wonder if you were eating yours too and what you were having. This love business, it's mad."

"Mad but good," I said, my eyes drooping.

"Definitely good." He kissed the top of my head.

The darkness didn't seem so creepy when I was with him, the struggle to get to sleep not a struggle at all. I was drifting, and it was as though tonight hadn't happened. We were safe as long as we were together, as long as he held me in his arms, and there was no other place I'd rather be—unless it was home but in the same place—bed, me pressed against him.

"I love you," he whispered.

I opened my mouth to answer, but sleep decided to pick that moment to steal me away.

Chapter Eleven

I woke with that blissful feeling of having nothing to worry about. A disembodied voice—which would normally have scared me shitless but didn't this morning—whispered that everything was hunky dory, thank you very much, and I could dance in the summer meadow of lushness that was life to my heart's content. It was a beautiful ideal, one I could gladly indulge in before it was time to get up. I snuggled further into the duvet, telling myself to go back to sleep for a little while—after all, we were on holiday where alarm clocks didn't exist—and catch up on some much needed rest.

Then the events of yesterday and last night kicked in.

I bolted upright, a lock of my hair slanting across my face like an unruly worm. I tossed it away and stared around the room. Yes, I was still in the hotel, and far from thinking all that lushness was waiting for me, I experienced only dread. What if Cauli had made up an excuse to the police, that he'd been forced to drive the getaway car or whatever? What if they had let him go and he came after us?

Bloody hell, this is a nightmare.

I turned over to face Leon. He still slept. I stared at him, hoping the intensity of my gaze would wake him so I had someone to talk to, someone to tell me everything would be fine. He snored softly, my mojo clearly not working on him, and I felt wretched for being so selfish in wishing he'd open his eyes. For all I knew he could have been up half the night, worrying about me, keeping watch in case someone knocked our door down and burst in, weapons at the ready.

Oh, for God's sake, shut up.

I got up to shower, dress and make myself presentable. Once I was as ready as I'd ever be to face the day, I tossed things into our cases, determined to get away from this place once we'd been to the police station to give our statements. The morning had the potential to drag on, fill me with more dread than I could handle and turn me into a nervous wreck. Or more of one than I already was. I shook from head to toes.

Pacing, I willed Leon to wake up. I needed his company, his calming influence. He didn't seem fazed by Cauli and the Gang at all.

The song *Get Down On It* sprang into my head — Kool and the Gang — and I cursed the way my mind played word association without my permission. Despite my annoyance, I danced, albeit half-heartedly, and sang along quietly.

"You gotta feel it, get down on it..."

Was I going insane?

Leon stirred, opened his eyes and caught me mid-twirl.

"Someone's happy today," he said, rubbing the sleep from his eyes. "Do you always wake up like this? I mean, I wouldn't know, seeing as we've never spent the whole night together before."

"No," I said. "I'm usually the groggy bitch from hell first thing, so be warned."

He groaned then propped himself up on his elbow. He looked adorable, hair all sleep mussed, and his skin looked as though it would be warm to the touch. I wanted to dive back into bed with him but the day's schedule wouldn't allow it.

"We have to go soon," I said on a sigh. "Visit the bloody station."

"Shit, yeah." He scrambled out of bed, gave me a quick kiss on the forehead then headed for the shower.

How could he have forgotten? Was he that blasé about the whole thing? Or maybe I was being overly dramatic. The title of Drama Queen didn't suit me because I didn't usually behave like one, but it seemed I'd soon be wearing the crown *and* the sodding fur-lined robe if I wasn't careful. Shit, I might even end up sitting on the throne.

While the shower did its thing with my beautiful man in it, I resisted stripping off and joining him. I wanted a hug, some form of contact, and this neediness that had sprung up since Cauli had entered our lives was getting on my damn nerves. Where had Pussy Pwoar gone, the woman who could cope with all sorts? I had to get her — or someone like her — back. Being whoever I was now wasn't one of my favorite roles. Mad Mandy had partially died the second I'd gone to bed with Leon. Part of Pussy had remained afterwards, and even Mrs Ponsonby had more balls than Just Mandy.

Leon came out of the bathroom, a white towel fixed around his waist and an appealing bulge between his legs.

I could just get hold of that and –

"Shit, time's moving on," he said, quickly getting dressed.

Whoever I was wanted to sulk. To rage that I didn't want to go to the station, didn't want to be involved in this crap. Scared Susan, that was my name, the personality I was this morning. And it didn't sit well.

We shot down to breakfast – a full English that should have been wonderful but tasted how I imagined dried sawdust would. It stuck in my throat each time I swallowed, and I pushed my plate away, still half full of bacon, sausage and a fried egg sitting on top of a lake of grease.

"Not hungry?" Leon asked from across the table.

"Not really." I smiled – didn't want to worry him – and looked around the dining room.

The tables were all full, diners chatting happily, probably looking forward to their stress-free day. I envied them. I should have been feeling like that. To stop myself becoming a Moaning Minnie – she was a cow and a half and appeared once a month at *that* time – I slapped on a smile and told myself that once the next few hours were dealt with, everything would be fine.

I'd gotten adept at lying lately, but even I had my limits. I didn't believe myself at all.

Breakfast over, we left the hotel and caught a taxi to the station. The reception area was empty apart from a policeman sitting behind a glassed-in desk. I idly guessed that the glass was reinforced to keep him safe from the nutbags of Blackpool, and as he listened to Leon explaining why we were there, I took a seat in the corner, away from the main door. An internal window set into the wall to my left revealed an open-plan office. People in casual clothing worked behind desks, and I supposed they might be the ones who typed up statements and did all the non-policeish things non-policeish people did when they worked in law enforcement. What they must read on a daily basis would be stuff fit for my nightmares and I wondered how they could do it without going batty.

Beyond the office was another window showing a corridor with several doors. All of them were closed and had silver plaques on. I reckoned we'd be going into one of them if they were detectives' offices.

Leon came over and sat beside me, placing his hand on my knee and giving it a bit of a pat. I linked my arm with his and leaned into him, comforted by his closeness.

"We'll be going through in a bit, apparently," he said. "They're going to interview us separately."

I hadn't thought of that. Leon didn't really know much so he'd be done and dusted quickly, but me? I groaned at the time I could possibly be kept nattering. Would I even remember everything in the right order?

"We're leaving once this is over, aren't we?" I cuddled his arm tighter.

"Yep, if that's what you want, although I really don't think there's anything to worry about. Maybe just move hotels?" He kissed my temple.

That would be better than nothing. "And not come out of it until it's time to go home."

"If you like. The rest of the week in bed sounds fine to me. Room service, champagne dinners — you up for that?"

I was and nodded. Perhaps I could be Pussy again, all sexy and wanton, ready to try anything and everything related to the rudies. I let my mind drift, imagined me bringing out some of the toys I'd packed, surprising him with my brazenness, pleasing him until he couldn't stand up straight.

A door beside the internal window opened and Detective Broadley poked his head around the jamb. "Morning. I trust it's a good one?"

Was he taking the piss?

"Oh," I said, straightening up a little, "if being scared stiff counts as it being a good one then I'm bloody ecstatic."

He cleared his throat, attempted a laugh but it failed, a gurgle down a dirty drain. "Right then, this way."

We followed him through the office and into the corridor. I glanced left then right, catching sight of a door that was ajar. Someone sat at a table facing the door—I made out their foot, leg and one arm—and they were drumming their stubby fingers on it. I swallowed, knowing it was Cauli—I recognized the jacket he had on. A silly little whimper came out of me, the kind I usually made when faced with a big fat spider in my bathroom. And my mind played word association again, throwing out images of Cauli being a tarantula and me being the fly.

I wanted to shit myself but refrained.

"You all right?" Leon whispered.

"He's in there." I pointed, hand trembling. "I didn't think we'd see him."

"Fuck it." Leon drew me close to his side. "Turn your back to him as we pass."

Detective Broadley continued to strut down the corridor. I wanted to stop, to squeal that I couldn't follow, but Leon tugged me on.

I should have done as he'd suggested, but of course I didn't. I stared through the gap as we approached, and Cauli leaned to the side to peer out. *Fuckshitcrap.* My insides turned to jelly and I found it hard to move on. He stared at me — minus the beard, a red rash in its place — with those piercing, evil eyes of his and lifted his finger-drumming hand off the table. He drew one of them across his throat and sneered.

I needed the toilet.

"Oh!" I said, a stupid response to match my stupidity in not hiding my face before he'd seen me.

"Watch it," he mouthed.

"Oh!" There it was again, a girly answer to a threat I could have done without.

I scuttled forward, so thankful the door was behind me, and raced into a room Detective Broadley stood in front of. A man sat behind a table and I was ushered away from Leon to sit opposite.

"We'll be next door," Broadley said.

I watched Leon leave with him, feeling so alone that I didn't know what to do with myself. Cry? Go after him? Scream?

"Are you okay?" the man asked. He stood, held out one hand. "I'm Detective Mattheson, by the way. And you're" — he checked a file on the table — "Mandy."

I nodded. "Yes. Yes, I'm Mandy, but no, I'm not okay. He's... That man...he's...he's seen me. That cauliflower-eared bloke."

"Pardon?"

"One of the robbers. He just saw me." I whittled my fingers in my lap.

"Oh, that's very unfortunate."

"The door was open and he...he bloody did this thing with his finger. Moved it across his neck like he was going to chop my head off. Then he...he said 'Watch it'. Oh, God, I feel sick."

"Calm down, Mandy. Give me two minutes, would you?"

He left the room, closing the door after him, and I stared around at the blandness, the off-white walls that were sullied by dirty fingerprints in places, the blue-painted wainscoting that was chipped and showed the wood beneath. The table reminded me of one in a school cafeteria, minus the plastic trays with their individual portion areas. I was a kid again, dragged back to childhood by a man and his cohorts, all without my consent.

Angry, I clamped my lips together. Who the hell did he think he was, terrorizing me like that, just because I'd had the unfortunate mishap to be in the wrong place at the wrong time? I swallowed bile and forced myself to stop fiddling with my fingers. The police would sort him, cart him away, and I could carry on with my life as though this had never happened.

The door opened. I jumped about an inch off my seat and whipped my head around. Detective Mattheson was back—*thank God it's him and not Cauli*—and I realized that I'd just been kidding myself. Anger wasn't enough to take away the fear. What if it stayed with me for the rest of my life?

Mattheson sat, picked up the file then tapped it on the desk. "I've spoken to the man in question. Now, if you could explain, from the beginning, how you came to know him?"

That wasn't going to wash with me. Sweeping this latest threat under the carpet would only mean that it was more dust added to an already large pile. I wanted answers before I gave him any.

"What did he say?" I stared at him, trying to show that he needed to be straight with me.

"He denied it, which isn't unusual in these situations."

I went to protest but he held his hand up.

"However, these rooms, as you can see" — he gestured to the left-hand corner — "have cameras, so there's no need to worry. Now, if you could begin?"

I relaxed a little, then recounted everything from the first time I'd seen Cauli to the last. It struck me that I'd probably have to do this again in court, and I'd run it through my head countless times before that too. Months of me thinking about this in one way or another stretched ahead and I wasn't sure if I could cope with it. It was obvious Cauli intended me harm, or to at least stop me from giving a statement and evidence.

"This gang," I said, "how...gangish are they?" I blushed at my word choice. I decided to try again. "How naughty are they?" And blushed again.

Naughty?

"We've been after them for quite some time." Mattheson stopped jotting in the file and looked up. "But if you mean will they have other people that haven't been caught who will obey their orders, yes, they do."

My whole body dove into panic mode. I got out of my seat and went for the door, wanting away from this bloody place and everyone associated with crazy, wicked thieves. I wanted to go home to my flat, where life had been predictable. Where I went to work, came home, snuck a quick visit with Leon, went to bed then did it all over again the next day. Keeping my secret from *our* gang had never seemed as banal as it did now. It wasn't a secret that should have caused me as much bother as it had. Not when I had another secret up my sleeve.

"I need to see him again," I said. I took a deep breath and prayed I couldn't get into any trouble for the things I was going to say in the next few minutes. "It's just that…" I paused.

What's the better option? Looking over your shoulder for the rest of your life, hoping a gang member doesn't come and get you, or looking over your shoulder thinking Cauli will?

I wasn't sure, didn't know if I could pull this off. I'd planned to lie, to say Cauli wasn't the man they were looking for, but now the words were waiting to come out… It was wrong to lie, to let them get away with it.

"Have other people identified him?" I asked, hopeful that was the case.

"Only by description. The identity parade comes later. You'll be home by then, but you'll go to your local station and watch a video."

Someone else could do the dirty work for you, pick him out, but he'd never know it wasn't you.

I sighed, knowing I may as well go with honesty. Whatever I did, Cauli would think I'd dobbed him in. I was stuck between a rock and a hard place — damn uncomfortable, that — and had to live with the consequences.

"Okay." I nodded, my bout of insecurity growing by the second. "Okay. So what if these people find me and Leon? What then?"

He smiled as though about to impart some devastating news. "We can't guarantee your safety, I'm afraid. We can only act when something happens. Preventing it… Well, things like permanent witness protection are only available in extreme circumstances. If you were to be threatened after you leave here, be told that if you give evidence in court you'll be harmed, *then* we can do something about it."

"So you're saying I have to go into the lion's den?" *Circle of Life* wailed through my head along with the image of Simba frolicking with Nala, insane smiles on their furry faces. Would Leon and I ever be like that again after this, or would Scar send someone to upset the balance?

"Unfortunately, yes. You'll have to continue as best you can. But the moment you're approached or telephoned, let us know immediately."

"Oh, I will do." Yes, I'd pick up that phone and screech down it until someone came and fixed things.

I gave my statement then.

"That's about it for now, Mandy." Mattheson stood, picked up his file and pen, then walked to the door.

I got up, full of trepidation. What if that other door was open again? What if Cauli saw me?

"It's quite all right," he said. "He isn't there anymore."

I sighed out my relief.

But he's still in my head and I can't ever see him moving out.

Chapter Twelve

The new hotel was rather swanky, all luxurious fixtures and fittings made to look gold. Burgundy was the theme, or variations of it, just like the casino, from the curtains, to the bedding to the carpet. I sank onto my back on the comfortable bed, grateful to feel safer but still secreting doubts in my mind. They were sitting on a big ship that was moored for the time being, but once the tide came in and they started sailing again, I might be done for. And being moored wasn't exactly a picnic. The boat still jostled, still lifted with the swells of the tide, always there, always letting me know I wasn't on solid ground. I could only console myself with thoughts that the ship was the *Titanic* and that every worry that was onboard would sink beneath the waves shortly.

"I want to hurt that bastard," Leon said, setting our cases beside a white dressing table with gold-colored filigree swirls on the Queen Anne legs. "I hate the way he's made you feel."

"I don't much like it myself, but what can I do?"

"It boils my blood knowing I can't do anything about it. Having my hands tied like this. Fucking stinks."

I draped one arm over my eyes, unable to bear seeing the look of desolation on his face. "I'd feel the same if you were scared. I'd want to help, make it all go away. I imagine anyone would be scared in this situation."

I smiled to ward off a case of the creeps that was threatening to attack me, little prickles of apprehension that nipped my toes and pledged to trample over every inch of my skin if I let my guard down. This wasn't on. How could I continue to live this way, Nervous Nellie with legs like jelly?

"Let's pretend this isn't happening." A surge of wanting to go back to normal went through me, taking me over with such force it surprised me and erased the prickles. Determination was a wonderful thing, the way it swooped to the rescue like a super hero in ball-busting Lycra and a flapping cape. It spurred me on, and my desire not to let someone else dictate how I felt went a massive way to making me feel braver. I sat up, straightened my shoulders and warned Cauli in my head that if he thought he could rattle me anymore he had another think coming. This girl wasn't going to be freaked out.

"Let's carry on this holiday like we would have before all this crap happened," I said.

My words hid a multitude of worries that still loitered despite my little internal pep talk, reminding me that we'd tried this before. And look what had happened. We'd been destined to attract some unhinged men who were up to no good. But I couldn't keep going over and over it. Nothing could change the past. If I didn't sort myself out, Cauli would win. I had to get past this shit.

"What, go out, you mean?" He raised his eyebrows and braced himself on the dressing table with one hand. "I don't want to put you in any more danger. Come on, you've got to admit being threatened like that, the way he did in the police station—it's pretty fucking mental."

"It is, but I bet the trial will be months away. Am I meant to stay indoors all that time? And going home isn't going to solve anything. If they're the type of gang who have mad connections... They could find me if they really wanted to." *Stop it. You're supposed to be forgetting about them. Him. What they could do.*

"But they don't know your name so how would they find you?"

I lifted my hands then slapped them down on my thighs. I shouldn't have let this conversation affect me in a negative way but already I'd failed. I'd have to give in to what else had been bothering me or go crazy. Better out than in, I supposed. If it wasn't swirling around inside my head, if I let the thoughts out, freed them, maybe then I could move on, even if only for a little while.

"They have ways and means," I said, feeling foolish for what I was about to say. "You've watched movies, haven't you? Seen the way they do it?"

"But that's movies, love." He came to sit on the bed, taking my hand in his. "They're made that way for a reason, to keep up the interest. Does anyone *really* send someone to your home town to do a bit of sniffing about in order to get your name and find you?"

It did sound fantastical but I'd read all sorts in the paper and...

"I don't know." I turned away to stare out of the window, a lump suddenly in my throat. *Damn it.*

The sky had gone dark gray, hinting at a coming storm, and wasn't that just a mocking portent? Wasn't fate just determined to make me think about this shit all the time? I sighed. There were storms to come all right, where I'd get soaked through from the rain and frightened of the thunder, paranoid that lightning would strike. But life went on, it had to, and while I was afraid now, surely it would ease off in the future. People picked up the shattered pieces of their lives and walked forward all the time. Why was I any different? I could do the same as them. Get a grip and be happy again. And there were worse things that could have happened. Cauli could have produced a real knife, held it to my throat and promised to jab it in if I didn't do as he'd asked. Or he could have pulled a gun on me, poking the business end of it into my temple, finger poised over the trigger, saying he'd pull it and blow my goddamn brains out.

Oh, God. Stop this. Please, stop this.

"Fuck it," I said, getting up and staring down at him. "We'll go out for dinner." That weird, whispering voice started up, telling me to get the hell back on the bed and stay there. I wanted to batter the shit out of whoever it belonged to. Mrs Subconscious Know-It-All or whatever she was called. She was trying to hold me prisoner, take over, and I was buggered if I'd let her. "Yes, we'll go out and bloody well enjoy ourselves." I mentally stuck my fingers up at her, pleased to feel her retreating, a stroppy air about her because she hadn't gotten her own way.

Leon failed at holding in a sigh. "In the corridor at the other hotel, Detective Broadley told me to be aware, to watch for anything strange, but other than that he said to behave as normal, so I suppose—"

"Well then." I smiled again, a fake one that hurt my cheeks. "That's what we'll do. Carry on as normal."

I rummaged in my case to pull out a dress that was crumpled from my frantic repacking earlier. It was a nice number, black and fitted, something that could pass for elegant yet casual, whatever the occasion required. Magazines said every woman should have a little black dress and at the time I'd bought it I'd *wanted* to be like every other woman. Now, not so much. I hung it on a hanger in the bathroom then switched on the shower. Hopefully the steam would iron out the fabric.

"We can pretend we're someone else again," I called out, tugging the hem of the dress so it hung straight. "Not Mr and Mrs Ponsonby. I was scared as her in the casino, although what she got up to with Henry in the bedroom is something I'll never forget. No, we'll be another pair of posh knobs. What about a couple who are spies and work for the government? We're indestructible. I'll be Miss Yummypenny. Who will you be?"

His laughter floated through to me as I stepped into the glass shower stall.

He came into the bathroom. I peeped around the misted screen to see him leaning against the wall.

"I don't know," he said. "What about Mr Wand?"

"Mr Wand?" I frowned, grabbing the shampoo and soaping my hair.

It took a few moments for him to answer. "Bond, except I'll be Jimmy not James. Jimmy Wand."

"Oh, for fuck's sake!" I laughed, so glad to feel more like my old self again. "That'll work, although you know I'm going to want to laugh every time I call you that."

"No more than I will, calling you Miss Yummypenny. She's older than him, like granny old. I'm not sure I fancy that." He grinned and it seemed some of the tension had left him.

I was so lucky to have him.

"No, not in our case," I said. "Yummypenny is Wand's young woman, more like the saucy tarts Bond fucks in the films. You know, all gorgeous tits and curvy arses. So, come here, Mr Wand, and show me your…wand."

Oh, that had been cheesy as hell.

He undressed quickly while I rinsed my hair, then he joined me, staring into my eyes. My stomach flipped as it always did when we were naked and close, and I waited for him to make the first move. He flattened his hands onto the tiles above my head, effectively hemming me in, but I wasn't about to go anywhere. He had me right where he wanted me—right where *I* wanted to be.

"So, young Miss Yummypenny, do you want to be shaken or stirred?"

"Both," I said, widening my legs.

He moved closer, pressing his hard cock into my pelvis. Wet skin on skin set my clit to throbbing, and I arched my back, pushing my cunt into him. His cock, trapped between us, hardened further, the heaviness of it a pleasurable weight. He pulled back a little then let his cock fall forward, butting the tip at my hole. Reaching down, he took hold of himself and rubbed his dick up and down my opening, circling my clit then repeating the motion from the start. I moaned, looking at him all the while, trying to gauge what he was thinking. Judging by the narrowing of his eyes and his concentrated stare he wanted to plunge inside me and fuck me so hard the tiles squeaked from my skin slipping over them.

The thought of that had me moaning louder.

"You like that," he said. "You like my wet cock on your wet cunt."

"Yes."

"The way it slides, the sound it makes."

"Yes."

"Me holding my cock—you like that too."

I nodded and bit my bottom lip.

"I bet you'd like to sit and watch me jerk off sometime, wouldn't you."

I found it difficult to breathe. His words, the steam...

"Watch me jerk off while you finger yourself. Yeah, you'd enjoy that."

I was being shaken all right, shaken by his words, by him knowing the kind of thing I'd thought about when we'd been apart. All that was left was to be stirred.

"But this"—he guided his dick inside me, pushing up until he couldn't fit any more in—"will have to do for now."

I gripped his waist, urging him closer, wanting all of him inside, every damn bit of him. He palmed my tits, massaging so my nipples perked, then he moved, in and out, slowly. I wanted fast—fast and furious—and whimpered with frustration. He smiled lazily, staring at me, his intense gaze snatching my ability to complain further. He knew he was in control and that I'd go along with whatever he wanted.

He kissed me, something else that was slow, and I held back any sound of complaint. If he knew how badly I wanted a frantic shag he'd tease me for longer. He pulled back, closed his eyes. Then upped his pace.

I could have cried out in victory but instead I took all that he was giving. Quick, sharp thrusts that brushed his pelvis over my clit. Hard pinches to my nipples that shot spears of lust down to my cunt. Scrapes of his teeth along my neck and onto my shoulder that forced ripples of pleasure to soar all over me.

"But this is what you really like," he whispered by my ear, forging in and out at speed. "This...is what...you really...fucking...like."

"Yes," I said, "yes!"

The top of my back slid against the tiles, and that sound I'd thought about screeched through the shower stall. I held his waist tighter, fingers slipping, thin streams of water gliding over them. A heavier torrent splashed between us, hitting his chest to bounce off and land on mine. His dick brushed inside me where my G-spot was—yes, it stirred me, *he* was stirring me.

"Fuck me, Wand," I said, imagining myself as a sultry Yummypenny, his sidekick, the one woman he needed to keep him on track. "Fuck me harder."

He sped up, bit down on my shoulder and went for it. He took me to another place, where only his cock ramming me and the bliss exploding in my clit existed. I channeled the pleasure, crested along with its waves, let my body do what it pleased, bucking and slapping the tiles, legs going weak. I lowered my forehead to his shoulder, watching his cock move in and out, hearing the squeak of the water and the loudness of his breathing.

"Yes," I said. "This is what I really like. You fucking me. Hard. Fast."

He bit harder, shuddering, stilling inside me for a moment before picking up his previous speed. I lowered my hands to his arse, held him like I never wanted to let him go. And I didn't. My climax ripped through me. I panted, still staring at where our bodies joined, loving him filling me, stretching me. He kissed my neck then my cheek and finally my mouth. I adored him the best way I knew how, with lips and tongue, roving my hands over his arse, clenching my cunt around his dick.

He withdrew his tongue to kiss my lips as he slowed his thrusts, peppering my face with light brushes of his mouth, and eventually he ceased moving. I circled my hands on his arse then lifted them to cup his face, to hold his head still. I looked at him, smiled, and a prickle of emotion hit the backs of my eyes. I traced a finger across his lips, up his cheek, over his eyelid, taking in every dip and swell of his features, the way his eyebrows were arched and so perfect, the way his lips were so full.

I loved him so damn much.

He reached for the soap and washed me while I just stood and let him do it, my hands splayed on the tiles either side of me. His hands, so warm and soft, lulled me into such a relaxed state that if I weren't in a shower I'd have fallen asleep. Him soaping my cunt had me opening my eyes, the sensitivity in my clit too much for it to be handled. He must have sensed that and withdrew his hand, urging me off the tiles to stand beneath the water so the bubbles were sluiced away. He washed himself, me content to watch him, to see how he did it so I'd know for the next time we showered together.

And there would be a next time, there was no doubt in my mind about that.

Chapter Thirteen

The restaurant bore all the hallmarks of being expensive. Luckily, my credit card had a few quid on it and I wouldn't be left red-faced when the waiter presented my half of the bill. I was determined to stick to my guns and go Dutch throughout our time away.

We were led to a corner that was private and secluded, surrounded by lush potted ferns with bushy, abundant leaves. I was glad for that. I could eat without worrying that someone was lurking nearby ready to make good on Cauli's threat. We were left alone to peruse the menu.

"What do you fancy, Miss Yummypenny?" Leon smiled at me across the table.

"Something light."

Our sexual encounter hadn't erased all the uneasiness inside me. My stomach was a bit dodgy, clenching every so often if a memory of what we'd been through flounced into my mind. I had a feeling that once we went back home and things returned to normal I'd settle better. Being in Blackpool, still so close to Cauli and the Gang, wasn't helping matters.

"Salad then?" He handed me a menu.

Salad wasn't usually my thing. I like hearty food, as my hips and arse showed off to perfection, but I thought it might well be the way to go tonight.

"Yes, chicken salad would be nice, thanks." I stared at the price. "But paying over a tenner for one is revolting. There must be something cheaper." I browsed the menu, startled to find that onion rings or a single slice of garlic bread were the only things below five pounds. "What is the food in here, gold-bloody-plated?"

"It doesn't matter." Leon pushed one of my hands off the menu and down onto the table. He covered it with his. "I'll pay, my treat. Tonight you're with Jimmy Wand, and he gets paid several thousand pounds a week to ponce around the city with gadgets and guns. He'll handle it, all right?"

I was about to protest but suddenly didn't have the energy. Still, when he ordered the salad, I cringed. Eating it would seem obscene, like swallowing money itself.

The waiter returned holding a bottle of white wine. I dreaded to think how much it had cost. He poured with practiced ease, not spilling a drop—and he should have been glad he hadn't too. One drop might equal fifty pence. I'd have been sucking the tablecloth in no time. He almost breezed away, disappearing into the main area of the dining room as if he'd never been near us. Now that we were alone, I relaxed my shoulders and told myself to push horrible thoughts from my mind and concentrate on enjoying myself.

Easier said than done but here goes...

"So, what's her secret?" I nodded at the woman at the table closest to us.

She was blonde, hair piled high in a glorious up-do that I'd never manage to copy. Her makeup, flawless, brought home the fact that I'd never be able to apply mine the same way without ending up looking like a woman overwrought with emotion after watching a soppy film. She'd used thick lashings of kohl—how it hadn't smudged I didn't know—and resembled someone from the sixties. Her dress, black and white, made up of four separate squares on the front, had me thinking of Mary Quant. She had flat black boots on, her legs bare and smooth and silky. Some people could pull off that look to perfection, and she did.

Leon glanced across at her then back to me. "Oh, that's eashee," he said, Jimmy Wand-Sean Connery style. "She's an undercover shpy like us. She's been sent to eavesdrop on our conversation and find out what we know. Later, she'll join us in the bar, where she'll have a Martini, shaken not stirred, and ply ush with the same so we get drunk and spill all our shhecrets."

"Then we'll have to make sure we don't, won't we. What about the man she's with?"

I looked at him sitting opposite her. Their body language spoke of more than a father-daughter relationship, and really, he wasn't that old now that I studied him more closely. Maybe he'd been unfortunate in that he'd gone gray early in life. She stroked his fingers that were wrapped around his wine glass stem and eyed him with blatant desire. Who the hell was I to judge? If they were happy, their age shouldn't matter.

I still had so much to learn.

Leon continued, "Oh, he's her mentor and she fell for him after they'd been working together for a week or so. Even though they're here on a mission, they wish they weren't. The hotel setting and whatnot. Makes them want to get a room — and if they go any further" — he jerked his head in their direction — "they might well have to."

I glanced their way again. She was running her foot up and down his calf. I blushed, giving Leon my full attention, biting my bottom lip.

"You could switch roles, Miss Yummypenny, and turn into Pussy." Leon gave me that stare of his that said he was up for playing games.

"I could, Mr Wand, but I rather like being Yummypenny. Anyway, as you know, she's a bit of a saucy mare herself, so Pussy isn't needed."

"So copy her," he said. "That woman. Do to me what she's doing to him."

I widened my eyes. "What, in here?"

"Yes, in here. Why not? It isn't anything outright rude. Just touching my leg."

"It's the other parts you might want me to touch that I'm worried about." I lifted my foot and grazed it up and down his leg. It was such a daring thing to do in a posh place like this. In The Rusty Nail, yes, I'd grab his balls in public if the situation called for it, but here? Yet I was doing it, undetected, no one any the wiser.

God, I loved bushy ferns.

"What parts did you mean?" He slouched down in his chair.

The toe of my shoe brushed his groin. "Oh! Those parts. And that wasn't supposed to happen."

"It was and it did. Carry on, Yummypenny."

I took a slow, deep breath and circled my foot over what felt like a glorious erection. "Good grief, Wand, shouldn't you go to the restroom and take out the banana in your pants, because it has to be a banana, it couldn't possibly be —"

"Be what? Shay it." He stared at me — hard.

I blushed hotter, looking around to make sure that the couple weren't listening. "Your wand."

"My wand?" he said loudly. "I don't have a wand but I do have a co —"

"Copious amount of wine to drink. Yes, you do, so finish what you have there and pour another." I glared at him, daring him to continue this way.

"Shpoilshport." He emptied his glass and did as he'd been told, refilling it to the brim. "More?" He tilted his head in question.

"Please, but I need to visit the ladies' room first." I got up, hanging my bag on my shoulder. "I won't be long." I stared down at the table. "Me being gone will give you time to deflate your wand. It's got far too much magic in it for my liking."

His chuckle followed me out of our little hideaway and into the main section of the restaurant. I headed for the foyer where there was a ladies' room in the corner by the main front door, smiling and thinking of the fun we were having as Wand and Yummypenny. There was potential for much amusement with those two. Staying in role, determined not to let Just Mandy's insecurities spoil the night, I pushed into the toilets — pleased to see they were clean and smelled of flowers — and chose the stall farthest from the door. Business done, I washed my hands then went back out into the foyer, thinking of how Yummypenny could do something sexual to Wand without it being obvious to other diners. Going under the table was an option, but if a waiter came along I'd be mortified at being caught giving a blow job. I wasn't that brave yet.

He could move seats, though. Sit beside me. Touch me up while I touch him up... Our hands would be hidden by the tablecloth.

I smiled at my plan and walked on into the restaurant, determined to act it out. I studied our corner, which really was well hidden, and knew that if we got up to the rudies no one would spot us — except for maybe the couple on the next table. They were still busy staring at one another. I peered into our corner, satisfied that if I couldn't see Leon from here, others wouldn't see us either.

A tap on my shoulder stopped me from going farther. I turned, expecting to see our waiter, but it was a tall, thin man in a suit, the one from the reception desk who'd greeted us when we'd come in.

"Pardon me," he said, "but there's a policeman here to see you."

I frowned. What the hell could Broadley or Mattheson want? I looked back at the potted fern in front of our table, thinking that Leon was playing silly buggers and had set this whole thing up. I wouldn't put it past him to have rung the desk and made up some silly caper.

"Oh, okay." I smiled and followed the man from the room and out into the foyer. Neither detective was there. "Excuse me." I patted the man on the arm. "Have they gone into another room or something?"

"I have no idea." He turned in a circle, his forehead streaked with deep lines, eyebrows raised. "A policeman was just here, I can assure you. One moment, please."

He went to the desk, picked up a phone and dialed. I got the jitters, wondering whether an officer had been sent to find us because... Because what?

The man finished his call and returned to me. "I'm afraid to say, according to our security fellow, the policeman left. I do apologize for disturbing you." He scanned the reception area. "Ah, there he is, out there, look."

I stared outside through the glass door. A uniformed officer was on a mobile phone, the peak of his hat shielding his face. He paced, not talking but listening to whoever was on the other end of the call. Perhaps he was waiting for Broadley or Mattheson.

"Would you mind letting my boyfriend know I'm out here?" I asked the man. "Only, he thinks I'm in the toilet."

"Certainly. The table in the far corner, isn't it?" He smiled, folding his hands over his concave belly.

"That's the one. Thank you."

I pushed open the door and went outside. The policeman stopped pacing, mumbled something into his phone then slipped it into his trouser pocket.

He smiled. "Mandy?" His voice was soft, had made him sound kind.

"Yes?" My belly rolled over. What was he about to tell me? I wanted to know yet didn't. It had to be something important for him to have been sent out to find me. And who knew we were at this restaurant anyway? Had Mattheson arranged for us to be watched after all?

"If you could just come with me," he said.

"Pardon?" I didn't want to go anywhere with him, not without Leon.

He grimaced. Looked up at the stars then back to me. He attempted a smile. "If you could just come with me..."

"Come where?" I wasn't sure I wanted to leave the relative safety of the restaurant, even though it *was* with an officer. "I'd prefer it if you came inside and spoke to me with my boyfriend there. I—"

"And *I'd* prefer it if you came with *me*."

He gripped my arm, tight and hard, and the first tendrils of fear set up home in my gut. I slapped at him to make him let go but he held on tighter. I looked back over my shoulder into the restaurant. The reception was empty and I cursed myself for sending that man off to tell Leon where I was. Then again, Leon might come out here, wanting to be with me.

"Get off!" I said, fight or flight taking over, some sixth sense kicking in. This wasn't right, and I wasn't about to go anywhere with him, officer or not. "Let me go!"

He squeezed my arm painfully then tried to drag me away from the building. "You'll do as you're fucking told, all right?"

Gone was the soft tone. He'd sounded far from kind just then, more mean and demanding. If he was an officer I'd eat my knickers. I yanked my arm, trying to throw him off, but he was having none of it. Instinct drove me and I kicked his calf, the pointy toe of my stiletto meeting muscle with a satisfying whack.

"I *said* get off!" I pulled my arm free and pelted away from him, smacking into the restaurant window in my attempt to get inside.

He came up behind me, securing my arm up against my back, and pressed me into the glass. "I only wanted a little chat, and you go and spoil it all."

"A little chat? Seems more like abuse to me," I snapped, anger and fear swishing around inside me, giving me false courage.

"So if you won't come with me, I'll just have to say it here, won't I?" He shoved me for emphasis. "We've been watching you, right, and we know your name, where you live, where you work."

How the hell? And so quickly?

I'd known Cauli and the Gang were more than they'd appeared. And if *I'd* known, just by what they'd done and the threats that had been made, why hadn't the police taken things more seriously? Why wait until something like this happened?

"So," he said, voice grating on my nerves and frightening me shitless, "what I wanted to tell you was that you'd better have a memory lapse, know what I mean?"

Oh, I knew what he meant, all right. "Yes."

"You *thought* you saw us. You *thought* you remembered who we were, but now you're not so sure. Got it?"

"Yes," I said, nodding, my cheek squishing on the glass.

"And if you don't forget us, and you tell the police what's gone on here, we'll find you again. We'll keep finding you until you push us to the point where we'll forget our manners and your life isn't important anymore. Understand?"

Despite having just been to the toilet, I had to hold my bladder. I nodded again. "Yes, yes, I understand. Now please, just let me go." I was trembling, freaked beyond measure and wanted nothing more than to get away from him. To be with Leon, safe.

"Make sure you *do* understand," he said, driving a knuckle into the back of my neck and pushing me toward the door.

That *hurt.*

I stumbled inside, crashing into the reception man.

"What the devil is going on?" he asked, setting me aside as if I were tainted. "Is she a felon? Do you need assistance?"

"A case of mistaken identity, sir," the 'policeman' said, his words not lost on me. "Isn't that right, Mandy? *Mistaken identity.*"

"Yes," I said, knees knocking.

"Oh, my dear." The reception man placed his arm about my back. "I do apologize for assuming otherwise, but we do get some rum types around here."

Rum types? Felon? What is he, stuck in the past?

Such a strange thought to be having in a situation like this, but I suspected that it was self-preservation, my mind asking questions that were easier to think about than those that waited in the wings to swamp me. Scarier ones. Evil ones.

"Let me take you to your good fellow," he said, guiding me away from the doors and into the restaurant. "He must have been in the toilet when I last went to find him. And what about what just happened, hmm? I tell you, it comes to something when even the police make mistakes. Good Lord, you ought to file a complaint."

"No, no, it's quite all right. An easy error to make." I concentrated on trying to walk straight.

"There," the man said. "Let's get you seated."

I plonked down into my chair, out of breath and feeling sick.

"What the hell's happened?" Leon asked, getting up to sit on a chair closer to me.

"Your good lady had a fright," the man said. "But I'm sure she'll be fine now. I'll leave you to it." He walked away shaking his head.

"Mandy?" Leon put his arm around me.

"They found us," I said. "They bloody went and found us."

Chapter Fourteen

We stood in the middle of a living room that was bland, furnished with thrift in mind. I supposed the police budget was strapped for things like this. Places like this. For people like me to hide in.

Us to hide in. Leon's with you.

An eighties sofa covered in brown hessian that looked like it would be itchy sat in front of the back wall. Two mismatched chairs—one a blue velour wingback with faded arms, the other a pea-green fake leather thing that swiveled on a silver foot that resembled a bird's claw—stood either end. A low, teak sideboard with chunky round handles that seemed as though it had been bought from a car boot sale rested against the left wall, complete with scratches and gouges from years of use. A coffee table topped with hideous yellow flowered tiles was at an angle in the center, like someone had knocked one corner as they'd walked past and hadn't bothered to straighten it. And the carpet... Bloody hell, it was worse than the one in the hotel corridor outside our room. It was all so dirty, so...flea-riddled.

I wanted to cry.

"It'll be all right," Leon said, putting his arm around me and stroking my hair.

A waft of cabbage swam past me and I wrinkled my nose, hoping Leon hadn't put on some new kind of cologne that had gone manky after a few hours. Although tidy, the house definitely wasn't a palace. Not only did it smell of cabbage, but there was an underlying scent of unwashed bedding in the air, as though hundreds of people had occupied the rooms and hadn't opened a window to let in any freshness. Maybe the windows didn't even open—maybe it was safer to keep them permanently closed.

The thought of that made me feel sick.

"No. It won't." I cringed at the tone in my voice. I'd sounded whiny, a little girl used to getting her own way and finding that this time she hadn't. Like Mrs Subconscious Know-It-All. "What the hell's happened? How can we have gone from visiting Blackpool for a dirty week away to this? We were supposed to be in that hotel, not standing in some manky safe house or other. And will it even *be* safe?" I huffed out a bitter laugh that bordered on sounding hysterical. "We thought we were safe in the second hotel and look where that notion got us." I could have kicked myself. "We should have stayed in, spent the rest of the week in bed, like you said. But I went and ruined it by saying we should go out, fuck the lot of them, and enjoy ourselves. Some enjoyment. I'm so sorry."

"Hey." He crushed me to him, holding my head to his chest, pinning me to him. "Think on what Detective Broadley said. It *will* be all right."

I had the need to move, to push myself off him, to pace and pace until I wore the bloody carpet out or got blisters. And Leon was stuck here with me, holed up in secret, our phones taken away and replaced with new ones that no one but the police had the numbers to. What a sodding mess. Our original secret had gotten so out of hand, and now we had extra ones to deal with. We couldn't phone home now even if we wanted to.

"You shouldn't be here." I stopped myself from crying, from screaming, railing at how unfair this was to him. "It's me they're after."

"Where else would I be?" he asked, heart pattering hard and fast beneath my ear. "Where else would I go, eh? Home? Leaving you here? Not fucking likely. We're in this together, all right? Always will be. Wherever you are, I'll be. Get used to it."

I sank into him, closing my eyes. Broadley had said we'd only have to stay here overnight or a couple of days at the most. The man from the restaurant reception had telephoned the police. I'd planned to do as I'd been told and not tell anyone what that fake copper had done and said. After all, what was yet another secret to add to my list?

We'd been ushered out of the rear entrance and into a waiting panda car, brought here and had it explained to us that we hadn't been followed and that one of Cauli's captured men had broken down and confessed to all they'd done. They weren't as big an outfit as I'd thought. The fake policeman was the only one left who hadn't been caught. No one else would be looking for me once he'd been apprehended. We just had to stay in this shithole while the police found him, that was all.

I'd be lying if I said I wasn't a bit relieved. I'd entertained thoughts of forever watching my back, worrying that some grimy *felon* was going to come along and grab me, take me to a hideout, treat me to some horrible torture then kill me.

"They've got a name for him," Leon reminded me. "They'll find him through DVLA records or something. See where he lives. Then we can go home."

And home was where I wanted to be. Right now, this second. With my eyes closed I could almost imagine we were there in my poky flat, where the air smelled of perfume and Glade Plug-In air fresheners, summer meadows on a brilliantly sunny day.

I will not cry.

"Tea then," I said, lifting my head and smiling. "My nan always said tea makes everything seem better. I bloody hope they have some in the kitchen. Milk, if they have it, it's bound to be off, unless the last people who were here left recently."

I went to investigate. The kitchen was as empty as mine had been on the day I'd moved in. I opened a cupboard, revealing crappy chipped crockery, none of it matching. The cups had tea stains inside that turned my stomach. The fridge was empty but I found a tub of dried milk in one of the upper cupboards. I moved to the sink, finding washing-up liquid and a scourer beneath, then set to work scrubbing the cups.

Buggered if I'm drinking anything out of them otherwise.

I was hungry — we hadn't gotten to eat our meal — and the small amount of wine I'd had wasn't sitting too well in my belly. A Chinese takeaway was being delivered at ten. The person who was dropping it off would apparently say a code sentence and only then were we to open the door. A policeman was sitting outside in his unmarked car, but still, Broadley had said we couldn't be too careful — we had to wait for the code. I hadn't been about to argue with that.

"They're clean enough now, love."

Leon's voice startled me and I jumped, dropping the cup into the bowl. Water splashed up, soaking my wrists, and I flung the scourer down. Tears came then, hot and fast as I realized how on edge I was, how downright bloody scared. I knew we wouldn't be found here, knew everything would work out in the end, but it didn't take away the fact that we'd been through a touch of hell in the past couple of days and had a bit more to contend with.

"Oh, come here." Leon held his arms out.

I ran into them, was enfolded in the biggest embrace and immediately felt better. He had the amazing ability of being able to erase the trials and tribulations, to help me find a measure of peace.

"Just imagine," I said, conscious of my wet hands dampening his top, "if the gang had more members and I was put here with a view to being taken somewhere else. Where I had to *really* become a new person."

"We, Mandy. *We* would have become new people. I'd give it all up for you. Our life back home, my job, our little gang. Everything."

"Oh, fuck." I cried in earnest at his kindness, his willingness to be with me no matter what. I'd dreamt of finding a man like him, thinking I'd never get one, and here I was, snotting up his shirt, staining him yet again with mess.

"That's it, cry it all out. I'm here."

There couldn't possibly be another man like him on the planet, could there? Out of all the billions there were, he was the top of the pile when it came to caring, loving and being supportive.

"We've been friends a long time, Mandy, and now we're lovers, a partnership. Stands to reason I'm going to stick around, doesn't it? What kind of man would I be if I left you in the lurch now?"

"An arsehole, like all the other men I've been out with." I hiccoughed, calming down, sniffing and knowing my face looked like a wet baboon's arse. Hideous.

He put his finger beneath my chin to lift my face but I pushed down so he couldn't.

"Don't look at me," I said. "I'll be ugly and —"

"I don't care." He forced my face off his chest.

I looked up at him. His eyes were glistening.

"I don't *care*," he said again. "All I want is for you to be happy. If you look less than your usual self it doesn't matter. Whatever you look like, you're beautiful to me. Overweight, slim. Pretty hair, greasy hair. Whatever, all right? You're mine and I love you."

My bottom lip trembled. If I wasn't careful I'd crumple into a madly crying heap on the floor. "You're too good for me."

He frowned and a dark expression took hold of his face. "Don't say that. Don't ever say that. *I'm* not good enough for *you*. If I was, that man wouldn't have pinched your arse in the first place. He'd never have followed you to the toilets. If I'd have been a better man I'd have met you at the door in the pub and walked you to the bar. Gone to meet you outside the toilets sooner. But I didn't, and now we're here in this crappy little house, all because we didn't want to tell our friends we were seeing each other. Well, no more. From now on we're doing it our way no matter what anyone else thinks. All that's important is you, us, and living our life the best way we know how. And that starts now."

I nodded, agreeing wholeheartedly — but still hoping I didn't look like that monkey's bum.

He wiped the tears from my face. "Go and have a wash. Put your pajamas on. I'll make the tea. The dinner will be here in a few minutes and I'll deal with that too. We'll watch a bit of telly on that stinky old sofa, cuddle up and pretend we've just moved in. Be a bit of practice for when we do it for real."

I smiled, looking forward to the day we did that. Choosing our home and what went in it, inviting the gang round for dinner and a game of Monopoly, laughing all night. Memories of this time away would be locked up, or if they weren't, hopefully looked back on with laughter, like it had all been some silly game. Perhaps that was the only way I'd be able to deal with it. By laughing. Joking. Exactly what Mad Mandy was good at.

He kissed me, long and hard and deep, and I pushed into him, wishing we were anywhere but here. Except we weren't and I had to deal with that. Sometimes life threw lemons so hard that the skin split and the juice squirted out into your eye. You were blinded for a bit, your eyes watered, then, although your eyes were still sore, you managed to see again. That was us—and we'd get through this shit.

I left him to go upstairs. My suitcase was already in the bedroom, and that was just as bland as the rest of the place. A bed, a battered mahogany wardrobe and an ugly chest of drawers. At least the bedding was clean and smelled of washing detergent not cabbage. Instead of a wash I took a shower—or what passed as a shower—using the gel that sat on the windowsill and washing off the touch of that fake copper. It took a while to get the shampoo out of my hair, what with the shower being more of a trickle than a waterfall, but surprisingly, once I got out I was refreshed and ready to face the world again.

It wasn't only tea that made everything seem better. Leon and water did too.

Downstairs, I sat on the sofa and ran my fingertip over the waffle material, mind wandering to places it shouldn't wander. I snapped myself out of the memories and smiled as Leon came in with two steaming mugs of tea. I wanted him to think I was okay.

"I washed the plates," he said.

"Thank you." I took the tea then settled back, patting the space beside me. The material did itch. "Like an old married couple, aren't we."

"I don't know about old, but married would be nice."

That was the second time he'd said that, and I wondered if that was his way of asking me or whether a proper proposal was in my future. He draped his arm over my shoulder and I leaned into him.

"Married would be lovely," I said. "Although I never thought it would happen to me. I imagined if it did I'd be older, when I'd grown up a bit." I laughed quietly. "Like I'll ever grow up. Who plays crazy games making up stories about other people? Who pretends they *are* other people? At my age too."

"We do. And we'll keep playing them until we're old and gray." He paused, then, "I bloody love you, Mandy. Best thing I ever did was going out that night years ago with Marshall. It meant I met you—and I knew even then you were special. Except Marshall said you were all friends, that seeing one another wasn't on the cards, and I respected that. Probably why me and you were worried about telling them. And then there's Gary. He went with Jen that first night we were together."

"It's just Marshall on his own now. Can't we find someone, fix him up?"

"We could, but you know how bloody shy he is. He's got to come out of his shell on his own. Maybe he will when he realizes how things have changed, how much they'll change in the future. I doubt we'll be going to the pub most nights, will we. We can if that's what you want, but nights in on the sofa — or in bed — are more preferable."

I thought of our life and what it would be like once we went home. "I only spent so much time in the pub so I could be near you anyway. And those other men — they were nothing, I didn't feel anything for them."

"I know exactly what they were. You scratching an itch."

I laughed. "Except none of them itched hard enough. They didn't give me what I wanted. And I didn't know *what* I wanted until we started seeing each other. God, me in that bloody corset that first night. What was I thinking?"

"I don't know, but I'm glad you put it on. Sexy little woman, you."

I lifted my face and waited for his kiss. It came, soft and beautiful, and for the time it lasted, I thought of nothing but him.

Chapter Fifteen

There was something to be said about spending the night and the following day together, alone. The only contact we'd had with the outside world was the Chinese delivery last night, a food shopping delivery from ASDA this morning, overseen by the policeman keeping watch in his car, and a phone call from Detective Broadley to say that we might well have to stay in the safe house a bit longer.

They hadn't found the fake copper.

I didn't feel too wonderful about that—who would?—but there was nothing we could do about it. We had to put our trust in the authorities—and that was something I found difficult. Trusting people with decisions I usually made wasn't my cup of tea, what with me being an independent woman and all that.

Beyoncé's warbling voice streamed through my head, and a snippet of Destiny's Child's music video joined it. I tried out doing Beyoncé's arse wiggle and failed. How the hell did she *do* that? Humming and arse-wiggling, determined to get it right, I moved about the alien kitchen, cooking dinner as best I could on an electric cooker — tricky, as I was used to gas.

"Nice to hear and see you're happier," Leon said from the doorway.

I squealed at him possibly having seen me dancing that way.

He took a seat at the little pine table against the wall. "I've hated seeing you so worried."

"Yeah, well, I've decided to try forgetting why we're here." I blushed and prodded a potato with the end of a sharp knife to check if it was cooked. "Don't get me wrong, I still think of it, but not in such horrifying detail." I turned to smile at him. "Mash or just boiled?"

"Depends how your mash is." He raised his eyebrows.

"Lumpy. I'm crap at it."

He stood and joined me at the counter. "I'll do it."

He drained the potatoes and I turned the pork chops under the grill. I got a glimpse of what it would be like for us to live together — and loved it. Harmony didn't occur between every couple, so I'd read in one of my many magazines. The amount of Dear Donna columns I'd browsed was enough to scare anyone off relationships. To have it like this, a quiet shifting of us working together with no need for conversation was nothing short of amazing. And novel. My conquests prior to Leon hadn't involved anything like cooking dinner. Those men had only been fuck buddies, really, now I came to think of it. There hadn't been anything meaningful about those relationships at all. I'd been searching for something they couldn't give. Who knew, they might be right for someone else, the perfect partner, but for me? No.

"I'm lucky to have you," I said, then cursed under my breath as a rogue globule of fat leaped from the grill onto the back of my hand.

"You are," he said, grinning, attacking the potatoes with the masher.

"You're not supposed to say that." I turned the grill down. "What you're *meant* to have said was, 'Oh, I'm so lucky to have you, dear lady. I can't imagine how I survived before you came along.' And then, even though we'd risk burning the house down by leaving the chops under the grill, you were meant to have abandoned those potatoes, grabbed me, bent me over that table there and fucked me stupid."

"Is that what you want?" he asked, pausing to look at me.

"It might be, but you'll never know for sure because you didn't answer me properly." I giggled inside.

He stared at me for a moment, probably weighing up what he should do next. I wasn't about to help him out.

You're a cruel mare sometimes, Mandy...

He switched the grill off. "I see. It's like that, is it?"

His eyes — oh, they had that sparkle in them — and I held my breath in anticipation.

"It is," I said, bracing myself to be hauled against his chest and kissed like I was the best thing on the planet.

"But what if I don't want to do it your way?" He clenched his fists.

Had he done that to stop himself from touching me? And that was another alien thing, a man having to hold himself back like that — and all because of me.

Bloody hell, you are lucky.

"Then do it your way," I said, brazen as you like, my tummy doing somersaults. I hid my hands behind my back—they were shaking—and my body was alive with excitement. What would he do next? What would he suggest?

Hurry, hurry, hurry…

"Take your clothes off," he said, staring, his eyes going hooded and sparkling with that glint again, only it was more intense, glitzier somehow.

I stripped, all the while wondering what the next few minutes would bring and, of course, thankful that I'd remembered to close the window blind when I'd come into the kitchen to make dinner. Giving the policeman outside a sex show wasn't on my list of jollies. And I wasn't sure if having sex knowing you could be seen was an offense.

I stood naked, the lowering heat from the grill warming the tops of my thighs. My nipples perked, and I looked him square in the face. He swallowed, darting his eyes from me to the drawers, and seemed to be making a decision.

What are you thinking? What do you want to do to me?

"If you don't want this," he said, "what I'm about to do, then say so."

"I don't know what you're about to do." *But I bloody well want to find out.*

"When I do it, this specific thing, you'll know what I mean." He closed his mouth and worked his jaw muscles. They pulsed under his skin. He stepped forward to drag his fingers down my cheek, then he held my chin between finger and thumb. "If you want me to stop, you have to say."

I was more intrigued than ever. His hold on my chin had me wet for him, too excited for words. I nodded.

"Bend over that table." He jerked his head to the side.

I widened my eyes, turned on that he was going to go with what I'd suggested but more so because he'd taken control. Being grabbed and flung over it was a fantasy that could wait for another time. This way, his commands had me on pins and needles. I thrummed with exhilaration. Him telling me what to do in such a…a cavemanish way—who'd have thought it would affect me like this?

Me Tarzan, you Jane.

If he said that I'd be lost, his for longer than forever. If he stripped off, baring his lovely torso, breathing deeply, his chest rising and falling. Oh, I'd swoon. I shivered from the delight of it all.

I turned my back on him to slide two chairs from beneath the table. A leg from each got tangled in the other and, impatient, I pulled them apart then set them aside. The wood of the table had been varnished and shone under the harsh illumination from the strip light. The surface was narrow, but there was enough space on it for what we were going to do—or what I suspected we would do. I tugged it from the wall a bit. I lowered my top half onto it—cold—then let my head and arms dangle over the rear side.

"That's it," he said. "Now you wait there a minute."

My breathing went erratic from an influx of pleasurable apprehension. My heart rate soared, and my cunt got wetter. He was shuffling about—the tinkle of metal upon metal had me thinking he was poking through one of the drawers. Had he hidden something in there earlier? And if so, what the hell could it be? His footsteps tapped on the linoleum, and I sucked in a breath, his body heat warming the backs of my legs and the curve of my arse.

He seemed to stand there for the longest time.

Something cold touched my bum cheek. I gasped.

"This," he said, "is what I was talking about."

"What is it?" I whispered, closing my eyes, trying to work it out. *Metal? No, not cold enough for that. Plastic?*

"A wooden spoon." He paused. "And I'm going to spank you with it."

That was unexpected.

But something I planned to welcome wholeheartedly.

"Do it," I said, lifting my arms so I could grip the far corners of the table. I knew I'd need something to hold on to, something else to concentrate on if the spoon stung too badly. "Go on, do it."

He lifted the spoon, leaving behind an imagined patch of heat where it had rested. It seemed to have branded me, although that wasn't possible. It hadn't been there long enough or with any significant amount of pressure to cause such a sensation.

He brought it down on my arse with a short whack. I jolted, air coming out of my mouth along with a grunt of surprise. I hadn't expected it to be so...so sharp.

"Oh!" I gripped the table corners tighter. Scraped my nails on the underside of the wood. Pressed my toes to the floor.

He smacked me again, harder, the connection bringing on a rash of stinging that spread from my arse cheek down to my cunt. I held my breath to better experience the burn, to feel with wonder how it affected me emotionally and my body physically. I liked it, wanted more of the same, and to discover that was like an epiphany. He'd untapped a need I hadn't known I had, and I told myself to relax while I went on this new journey, to take it all in and store it inside my head, for no new thing was the same the second or third time around.

"More," I said.

He obliged. Each strike intensified the heat on my skin and it seemed that my flesh undulated, creating a ripple effect from the struck site to my cunt, much like the waves of the sea. They rolled, swelled, then crashed throughout my folds, ending their motion at my clit, where they tickled and teased, promising so much but retreating just before they delivered.

Maddening.

"Please, more," I said again, wanting that ripple to have no stopping point, for it to go on and on so those brief tingles in my clit were never ending and had a chance to grow into something of more substance.

I wanted to see if I could come just from having a piece of wood slapping my arse.

He worked on, his breathing labored, alternately tapping softly then hitting pretty hard. I imagined his excitement growing right along with mine. I needed to turn or to at least peer back to see what his face was like. Were his features full of concentration? Was his cock hard? Yet at the same time it was divine to just rest where I was, allowing what he was doing to roll over me, take me wherever it had a mind.

The shudders between my legs grew, as did the heat on my arse cheek. That was on the verge of sending my skin numb and it prickled from being so hot. It wasn't the pleasure-pain of the stinging strikes I wanted, though, but the result they made. And that result was right on target now, those slight tickles from before changing into something more electric, more intense. My clit hardened as it swelled, then throbbed, an aching beat that was unbearable and wonderful in equal measure. I chased my goal, loosening my grip on the table. I was draped there, his to do whatever he would with, and that was the icing on the cake.

I trusted him—totally.

"Oh, God, I'm nearly there," I said breathlessly, unable to finish what I'd intended to say. I knew coming just from this wasn't going to happen—I needed something else. Him. "I...I need... I want..."

I widened my legs to let him know what I wanted. He continued with the spanking, plunging what felt like all of his fingers inside me, stretching me wide, the width of his hand wedged tight against the sides. He curled the ends of his fingers. My hole widened a bit more to accommodate the intrusion, then a riot of pleasure had my channel rhythmically clamping around his hand. He rubbed my G-spot, rapid strokes that brought on the need for me to cry out, the touch seeming too sensitive, too much. I was on the verge of asking him to stop but the strange feeling down there changed into soft bliss. I jutted my arse out, shoving my cunt farther down his hand, writhing with my need to be handled, for everything to be touched at once. The ripples combined with him moving his fingers sent me on my way.

I came, jolting, breaths as hot, short and erratic as the wooden spoon smacking my arse. I rode it out, body feeling boneless, my mind spinning with everything and nothing at all. Time passed with me floating, him smacking and rubbing, until I whispered, "No more. Please, no more." Spent, I went still, panting, zoning in on the dull thuds of my clit.

Leon stopped spanking, withdrew his fingers then turned me over, sitting me right on the edge of the table. I put my hands behind me to hold myself up and looked at him standing there, wooden spoon still gripped in one hand, the fingers of his other wet.

"Fuck," he whispered. "Fuck."

He dropped the spoon then wrenched open his jeans. He tugged his cock out from the slit in his boxer shorts, handling it roughly, as though he couldn't wait to get going. Out of breath, all I could do was watch while he came toward me then stood between my legs.

"You," he said, "are a beautiful little... Shit, I want to fuck you."

He pushed in and I gasped at the swiftness of it, loving how he fitted there so perfectly. I hung my head back, exposing my neck, and let him fuck and fuck and fuck. I raised my legs, crossing them at the ankles behind him, driving him deeper. He flattened his hands on the table beside me for leverage and went for it. Each thrust, each withdrawal, each primal growl he released sent me closer to a second orgasm. The table shifted, the legs screeching on the floor, adding a rough and ready quality to our fuck. And that was what it was, a fuck, plain and simple.

And I loved it.

He bent his head to kiss my neck then sucked the skin over my collarbone, hard enough to leave a mark. The thought of it being there only for us to see, hidden beneath my clothing, a reminder of what we'd done, ratcheted up my need for him.

"You sexy bitch," he said, pushing in roughly, sending the table sliding backwards to slam into the wall.

I closed my eyes, pleasure barreling into me, through me. His cock stiffened then throbbed, and wet heat flooded my cunt. An orgasm flowed through me, one that didn't hold the strength of before but a lighter, all-consuming swaddle that carried me away. I moaned through my pleasure, a long, drawn-out sound, and listened for the same to come from him. There it was, telling tales that he'd reached the peak of his pleasure. He shuddered, pushed in on a long stroke then stilled.

I lifted my head to look at him. His eyes were closed, his jaw rigid, and sweat had beaded at his temples. I sighed out my utter completeness, that feeling unknown to me until I'd first had sex with Leon.

And I knew, deep inside me where my soul was singing with the strength of a full choir, that I'd never feel like this with any other man.

Chapter Sixteen

Two more days passed, as did four more phone calls from Detective Broadley. I was experiencing a huge bout of cabin fever that whispered of sending me insane. I was used to going out when I wanted to and not being restrained. The fact that I *couldn't* go out seemed to make it worse. The choice had been taken away and that's what bugged me the most. Because of Cauli, other people were directing my life and I hated it.

I paced the bedroom, looking around at the bare walls where pictures, a mirror or wallpaper should have hung, anything to break up the monotony of white, white, white. And grubby white at that. I supposed they had a cleaner who came in to give the place a once-over when people left, but they either weren't paying her enough or she was a lazy mare. I wondered if she even knew what this house was or whether she assumed that it was let out on a nightly basis. Did she even care? Would I in her shoes? Yes, I would have entertained all sorts of scenarios. My imagination wouldn't have had it any other way.

A light film of dust coated the off-white paint on the skirting boards, like the vacuum cleaner was ancient and it spat out more dust than it sucked up. The dressing table had a chipped corner where compressed wood chippings peeked out from the surrounding plastic coating. Very shabby, but really, what did I expect? This wasn't meant to be The Ritz. The stool in front of the dresser was like one inside a pub, the brown material-covered foam on top flattened from so many arses sitting on it. It brought The Rusty Nail to mind and I smiled.

The smile soon faded. How many women had sat there, frightened out of their wits? How many women had stared into the mirror, seeing someone they hadn't seen before, a face that was theirs yet wasn't?

I dreaded to think.

Leon turned over in bed, the mattress making an alarming creak that spoke of the bed base possibly giving up the ghost in the very near future. I didn't know how he could sleep so solidly on it. The mattress was lumpy and had a dip in the center that meant however hard we tried we rolled into it, forced to sleep squashed together. Not that I minded that.

I envied him his oblivion. I hadn't slept well at all here, which wasn't surprising, considering what had been going on and what still went on in my head. The latest from Detective Broadley, which had come last night, was that they were closing in on the suspect. Their net was all around him. All that remained to be done was them dragging it closer to shore, him caught up in it so tightly there would be no means of escape.

Naughty people were tricky to catch, though, weren't they? They knew all about nets and how to get out of them. All about hiding below radars. Slippery fish, the lot of them.

I shuddered and went to the window, parting the curtains a little bit, making sure to stand so the shaft of sunlight didn't sprawl itself on Leon's face and wake him. Netting was up, again something that could do with a good wash, and I narrowed my eyes to peer through the greyness of it. There was a slight tear in the fabric, giving me a thin slit to look through.

Despite the coldness of the season, the sky was blue and cloudless, giving off the lie that it was nice and warm out there. Frost on the grass told a different story. A tiny icicle or two hung from the branches of a large, naked oak tree in the front garden. Those branches seemed to stretch out, twiggy fingers intent on stroking the glass, at getting hold of me and not letting go. Someone walked over my grave, and I turned my attention away from the tree before my imagination went into major overdrive.

The houses opposite were gray brick on the bottom and decorated with pebbles wedged into cement on the top half. Between those was a line of red tiles, creating a border. It was a really odd combination, and they looked like two pieces of very different cake with jam in the middle. Each door was painted, some dark green, others red, a couple black. The front gardens were square patches of grass surrounded by dark wooden fencing, the half-diamond tops doing a bad job at being a much sought after picket fence. Plus, they weren't white. And that was the ideal, wasn't it, that white picket fence? It represented happiness and stability. Somewhere you could rest and be safe.

An unmarked police car was still parked at the curb directly outside. The plain-clothed officer in it appeared to be on the phone. I couldn't see his head, but one arm was bent in the position it would be in if he were chatting on the blower. He gestured with his other hand then jerked a thumb at the house. My stomach didn't like that, bunching tight so that bile zipped up to paint the back of my tongue. I swallowed, fighting off the shakes that seemed to want to envelop me.

I hate this…this bullshit. Being here. On edge.

He talked for a little while longer then got out of the car, slipping his phone in his suit jacket pocket. He glanced up and down the street. Seemingly satisfied no one was taking any notice of him or hiding in the bushes of the neighboring gardens, he walked around the car then onto the pavement. He paused at the weathered wooden gate, his hand hovering above it, and cocked his head. Whatever it was that bothered him, he ignored it and unlatched the gate. He strode up the path then disappeared beneath the porch roof.

I held my breath.

The doorbell sang its gaudy tune, one that went on for far too long and got on my nerves. I rushed to the bed, jostling Leon awake.

"The policeman from the car's at the door," I said. "Quickly, get up!"

I raced downstairs, almost tripping on the last step in my haste to let him in. He had to have news—good or bad, it didn't much matter at this point. Anything he said would break this monotony of being trapped inside, giving me something else to either shit the life out of me or make me feel better.

I turned the three keys in the locks then jabbed the code into the alarm pad beside the door. It beeped and another internal lock snapped open. I hunkered down to peer through the letterbox. I couldn't get those damn movies out of my head. Anyone could have grabbed him off the porch and be standing there instead of him. I was greeted with the sight of his groin area, the weave of his suit trousers fine with a silky appearance. I blinked, sure that it was him, and stood upright to open the door a couple of inches, the security chain preventing it from gaping fully.

It *was* him.

He smiled as I sighed, unthreaded the chain then let him in.

Seeming to fill the narrow hallway, he closed the door and leaned on it.

I stared at him, waiting for whatever it was he had to say.

"They've got him," he said.

I sagged against the wall. He reached out a hand to catch me if I fell but I didn't. I pressed my back to the wall and looked up the stairs at the sound of Leon coming down. I couldn't see him, my vision had blurred, and a tear rolled down my cheek. I wanted to sob, sob and sob until I choked, but now wasn't the time. I swiped the tear away and steadied my wobbling lips.

"They've found him," I managed, wanting Leon to hurry up and get his arse to me where he could hold me and stroke everything bad away.

"Thank fuck for that." Leon rounded the newel post and came to me, hugging me to him.

I reached up to fist his T-shirt, the material so soft on my skin, and again resisted the urge to cry.

"Yes, sir," the policeman said. "This morning. Early. He'd been hiding out at a friend's place. Doubt he'd been expecting us, thinks himself above being apprehended, that one. But early morning raids always catch them out, see."

I was sure they did, and the films and documentaries I'd watched proved that. Coppers banged on doors with the sides of their fists, shouting 'Police!' then opening the doors with metal rammer thingies if the occupants wouldn't open up. Oh yes, I could see it all, them doing that then bursting in, the lot of them fanning out inside the house to finally find the sneaky little bastard cowering under the bed. Not so macho then were they, those criminals. Well, those in documentaries weren't, but the ones in films? A fight would have broken out, the crim thumping, kicking and stabbing his way free, out onto the street where he'd be pursued on foot. Or maybe, if he got away in a car, there'd be a chase complete with a helicopter tracing his getaway route.

"Did he go quietly?" I asked, thinking he might well have. He could have snatched me outside the restaurant, dragged me away and held me hostage, but he hadn't. He'd seemed as though he didn't have the balls.

"He did," the policeman said. "Now, I just need you to sign some forms to say you're leaving here. I'll also take your addresses again. I know we have them at the station but it's best to be sure. Then you can go home — or stay here for the rest of your week, up to you."

I looked up at Leon.

"We're going home," he said.

I wasn't about to complain. I'd had enough of this house and Blackpool in general. I didn't think I'd ever return. A shame, because there was nothing wrong with the place. Just the memories it held.

"All right," I said, moving away from Leon and toward the kitchen door. "Would you like tea while we go through the forms?"

Because tea… *No, it's time to stop believing that. Face reality. You have shit to deal with long after you get home and tea isn't going to make any of it better.*

"Please," he said. "If you wouldn't mind. The coffee in my flask went cold hours ago."

I felt bad then. The poor man had been stuck in that car all night. It had been a cold one too. I wondered, as I went into the kitchen to flick the kettle on, whether he'd had a blanket of some kind or thermal coat and gloves.

"I'm sorry you had to babysit us," I said, unable to look at him. Instead, I took the milk out of the fridge then busied myself putting tea bags and sugar into cups.

"All part of the job."

A chair scraped on the floor, then another, and I assumed Leon and the policeman were sitting at the table. A flush spread over my face at the memories of what we'd done there. Was Leon thinking the same thing?

Leon cleared his throat.

He must be…

"So, if you could read these through, sir. And here are your phones. Of course, I'll need the others back."

The shuffle of paper sounded then was swallowed up by the gurgle of the kettle and the snap of it switching off. I made tea then placed the cups on the table. I sat and Leon passed me the forms. I read through them, filled out the relevant parts with the pen the policeman handed to me, and signed on the dotted line. We were free to go home, to get out of this strange little house that was supposed to act as a home but had failed miserably.

While Leon and the policeman chattered about football, I thought about the many memories these walls held, the things that had gone on in here. The people this house had sheltered — were they okay now? Had their worries passed, enabling them to continue their lives in peace? Or were they still effectively running, re-housed in other safe places with new identities?

"How long will they be put away for — if they're put away?" I interrupted. "Sorry. I should have waited for you to finish but I —"

"That's all right," the policeman said. He tilted his head in thought. "It's difficult to say, really, but if these are the people we think they are, it could be for quite a while. There are other things we think are down to them. So, bail won't be posted, because as you can imagine, us letting them out before trial when there's proof that it *was* them who robbed the bank and shot that woman…"

Relief went through me on Olympic running shoes. "Security cameras?"

"Among other things, yes." He smiled. "So you have nothing to worry about for, what, about fifteen years?"

I could handle that. "Thank God…" My lips trembled again — bastards — and I stared at the tabletop. If I looked at Leon I'd end up a sniveling wreck. "And we'll be informed of the video e-fit, the trial?"

"You will. I probably shouldn't be saying this, but in your circumstances it might be better if you didn't give evidence. You don't need to, really, what with the information we already have. You being threatened… Well, talk to a lawyer — they'll advise you on what's best. But I wanted you to know your testimony won't alter a positive conviction, so what's the point putting yourself through it?" He sniffed. Got up to take his cup and put it in the sink. "Broadley will have my bloody arse if he knows what I just said."

"Pardon?" I turned to fully look at him.

"I'll wait while you gather your things," he said. "Then take you to the station to collect your car."

"I'm grateful, really grateful." I stared at him to convey I'd meant him telling us about the evidence and not that he was taking us to the station.

He nodded. "I'll wait in the hallway." He picked up the forms then slid them in his pocket and left the room.

Finally I looked at Leon. "We're going home," I whispered.

He smiled. "And we're putting all this bollocks behind us, all right?"

I nodded, stood then slid the chair beneath the table. Leon did the same with the others. We stood there in that odd little room and hugged one another. This house had seen me secretly crying at night while he'd slept, me not wanting to worry him as to the extent of my fears. This house had read my thoughts and sucked them out until frightful images had danced in the darkness above my head, cavorting as though egged on by devils. And this house wasn't going to see us again, would be cleaned—as such—and sit empty until the next scared person walked through the front door.

I pulled away, wiping tears I hadn't known I'd shed, and smiled a wonky smile.

"So," I said, my voice a bit shaky, "we'd better go and pack."

"I love you," he said. "You're the bravest woman I know."

I didn't answer—couldn't manage it—just smiled and left the room, afraid that if I didn't I'd have a complete meltdown. I didn't want him having to help me out of it, for him to see me lose the plot like that.

I walked past the policeman with my back straight, my smile still in place. Climbed the stairs. Went into the bedroom. Sat on the bed and stared at our open cases on the floor. The clothes were a jumbled mess, tangles of arms and legs that reminded me of my emotions.

Brave on the outside, yes. But on the inside?

The answer to that was a secret I planned to keep to myself.

Chapter Seventeen

The Rusty Nail had never seemed so bloody lovely.

I stood inside the doorway and sniffed the air—beer, perfumed or cologne-splashed bodies, the still-lingering remnants of cigarette smoke from years ago.

I was home.

Jen stood at the bar with her arms wrapped around Gary, snogging his face off while a bewildered-looking Marshall stood there awkwardly, clearly unsure where to put himself. I smiled, really smiled for the first time since we'd been back, and shook off the melancholy that had settled over me on our journey home.

I'd allowed myself to entertain thoughts I shouldn't have. About Cauli and the Gang, what they'd done, what he'd said to me. It was inevitable, I'd told myself as the countryside had skipped by Leon's car in a blur, that I would have dissected it all again. One last time, I'd muttered, one last time then I'd put it behind me for good.

Now I felt I could. Being here, in the place I spent so much time, with people I cared for and who cared for me — yes, that would be my salvation.

And Leon.

The door creaked and I turned to see him coming in. We'd driven straight here from Blackpool and he'd parked around the back. I'd wanted to test my mettle, choosing to walk from the car park and into the pub by myself, in the dark. I'd been fine. I hadn't imagined anyone waiting to ambush me, hadn't scoured the street for signs of madmen wielding guns, running out of the bank toward me. Everything had been as it should be. People walking the pavements, cars puttering along, the street lights lit, casting their amber glow on the ice-speckled ground.

Things were going to iron out, I was sure of it.

"All right?" Leon asked.

"Yes. Why shouldn't I be?"

He cocked his head. "I won't answer that. It's just you were a bit quiet on the way home. I worry about you, that's all."

"No need." I took his hand in mine. Smiled up at him. "Ready?"

"As I'll ever be." He took a deep breath then led the way toward the bar.

Marshall nudged Jen, who broke her face-swallowing kiss to turn and look at us.

"Mandy! You're back early," she shrieked, throwing herself at me, almost knocking me flying. "You cow! You turned off your phone. I've been so worried." She hugged me tight then stepped back. Then she turned to Leon. "And you did too. Turned off your phone. What the hell's the *matter* with you two? I mean, Leon, you can get away with it because you'll have been working, but you?" She focused on me and let go of one hand to poke me in the chest. "You have no excuses."

Oh, I did, but oddly, I didn't want to tell her about them. This would be the second secret I'd keep from her. The first I was about to reveal, but the one where Cauli featured... No, that could stay firmly locked away. It was too frightening to relive.

"I did have an excuse," I said, going back into Mad Mandy mode, the woman she'd expect me to be and the one Leon had suggested I revert to when telling our gang about us. "Didn't I, Leon?"

"You did," he said, winking.

"All right, mate," Gary said, Marshall saying the same. "Have a good time, did you?"

Leon nodded, his smile a mile wide.

"Hang on a minute," Jen said, ushering me closer to the bar and the others. "What do you mean you had an excuse? Those two there interrupted." She threw Gary and Marshall a mock filthy look.

I stared around at them all, then at Leon. He nodded.

"Me and Leon have been shagging," I said, hating that term, hating the way Mad Mandy didn't fit me anymore.

She was crass, someone I'd turned myself into so I could hide my real feelings. She didn't belong to me anymore, not now I had Leon. There was no need for me to act the ladette, tossing vodka down my throat as easily as I'd tossed men off. I'd softened, become a woman with tender feelings instead of raw ones, the need to pleasure instead of being pleasured.

I was different, a new woman. Or the woman I'd really been all along, someone I'd buried beneath too many personas so that my real self had become lost. I was Just Mandy forever now, the girl who had a steady relationship, who didn't need to get drunk and have sex with strangers or make herself out to be the life and soul of the party.

"Shagging?" Jen shouted, drawing attention from other customers.

"Shh!" I said, blushing—something I'd rarely done in front of her.

"You dirty pair of buggers," she said. "Since when? Blackpool?"

I was tempted to stick to our plan, to say that we'd met up there and had hit it off as more than friends. But something inside me told me not to. It wasn't the weird voice from Blackpool. It was my soul.

I looked at Leon. He shrugged.

"No," I said. "Before that. For months."

"What?" Jen pranced up and down. "How come you didn't say? Why didn't you tell me?"

Gary barked out a laugh. "Probably for the same reason you didn't tell her you've been seeing me. Privacy. Something to call your own." He paused, looking from me to Leon in turn. "You two having your usuals?"

I nodded. While Gary ordered our drinks, Jen dragged me toward the ladies' room. I didn't want to go, not down that corridor where...

I allowed her to take me, eclipsing the horrible memory with the one where me and Leon had fucked in the cellar. That was how I'd handle this crap from now on. Every time a nasty reminder tried to slap me in the face, I'd beat it away with a happier one—one that didn't involve Cauli and the Gang.

In the toilets, Jen pushed open all the doors to make sure we were alone. She rammed her hands on her hips and tapped one foot on the floor tiles. "Dish."

"I don't want to," I said, surprised at myself.

"What do you mean you don't want to? Fucking hell, I've got so much to tell you it's unreal. Shall I go first?"

She went into a cubicle, shut the door, and proceeded to do her business, waffling all the while about her and Gary. I smiled at the animation in her voice.

"He has the best willy I've ever seen, Mand. Seriously, the biggest *ever*! And the things he does with it. Oooh-ee!"

I laughed, caught up in her tale but already missing Leon. I realized that I didn't want to be away from him for any length of time. Glued to his side, that's what I wanted to be. Yes, I knew that wasn't possible or even healthy, but it was what it was.

Jen burst out of the stall, going to the sink to wash her hands. She prattled on, shoving her fingers beneath the automatic dryer, the hot air blowing her hair around in a wild, gyrating mass of locks. "And when he went down *there*. Oh. My. God! Let me tell you—"

"No," I said, holding my hand up. "Don't tell me. I don't want to know."

"But we've always shared everything," she said, looking at me over her shoulder and frowning. She dropped her hands to her sides. The dryer went off, leaving behind a deafening silence. "Mandy?"

I smiled, yet another wobbly one, and shrugged. "Some things... Some things are better not shared, you know?"

She leaned one hand on the sink surround. "What, so you're not going to dish the dirt on you and Leon?"

"No. I want... No."

Her face clouded for a moment before the sun shone again as she masked whatever upset she'd felt. "Like Gary said. Privacy?"

I nodded. "It just doesn't feel right."

Her mouth dropped open. "Shit." She shook her head in wonder. "You're in love with him, aren't you? Like, this is *real?*"

I nodded again. I didn't want to share—not any of it. Those things belonged to me and Leon, no one else.

"Bloody hell," she shrieked, "that's great!"

Enveloped in her fierce hug, I stumbled backwards, laughing with her, relieved that she'd gotten the picture without taking offense. Eventually she let me go, let me breathe.

"When's the wedding?" she said, gripping the tops of my arms and giving me a look that said she'd been joking.

"I don't know, but I think it'll be soon. We haven't set an actual date. Just talked about it. He hasn't asked me officially, just said he'd like to marry me. Casual conversation kind of thing."

"Oh, my God, that's so brilliant!"

Jen's squealed words meant that she'd go on and on if I didn't get out of there.

"I have to go back," I said, pushing open the door. "To him."

I raced up the corridor and into the main pub, bypassing the table me and Jen used to sit at, a thousand memories flooding my brain. Our old life, the way I used to act, the feelings I'd held inside, secret, something I'd never thought Leon would ever know. More of our old life but the true start of us being together, me and Leon in Blackpool, hiding out, afraid, with only each other for comfort. And our new life, the future, with every bad memory filed away, us content and happy.

He was there, at the bar, a pint in hand, held midway to his mouth. He saw me and lowered it, staring across as though he hadn't seen me in years. Our surroundings melted away for me, leaving only him in my sights, his smile, the glint in his eyes, the silent question 'Are you all right?' floating between us.

I nodded and walked to the door, catching sight of his frown as he looked from me to our drinks. I shook my head, pushed the door open then went outside. The air cooled my skin, prompting me to lift the collar of my coat to ward off the chill. I stared up at the moon, at the stars, and thanked my lucky ones that I had met a man who'd enabled me to become myself, a woman who was comfortable with who she was. That I had demons to slay was something I'd deal with, Leon by my side, but I'd kill them, banish them for good so long as he was with me.

The pub door creaked and I smiled.

"I felt the same," he said, coming up behind me and crossing his arms over my front. "I don't belong in there anymore."

"It wasn't right. I'm not the same person I was." I leaned my head back onto his chest. Watched a few stars twinkling. "I don't fit." I paused. "And I'm glad I don't."

"We could go in once every so often, to catch up." He hugged me tighter. "Maybe a Sunday lunchtime when there isn't the expectation to get rat-arsed. That kind of life is behind me now. Can't believe I ever lived it, to be honest."

I knew what he meant. "Bloody hell, what were we *doing* back then?" I cringed at the thought of my many conquests. Faceless men I probably wouldn't recognize if they stood before me now.

"Living, getting to know ourselves. Trying to find a place that suited us. Isn't that what everyone does?"

"I suppose."

"Want me to walk you home, make sure you get back okay?" He kissed the top of my head.

"No, I want you to come home with me, stay with me." I turned in his arms. Pressed myself to him. "I admitted to Jen I was in love with you. That we'd talked about marriage. It felt wrong to say it, for her to know something like that, as if it's something only we should know. Is that weird, me wanting to keep our business a secret still?"

"Not if that's what makes you happy. I've told you before, you do whatever makes you happy. It's all I want."

I stared at a couple walking down the path toward us. They were holding hands, swinging their arms. She was talking and he threw his head back and laughed. I didn't envy people like that anymore.

"What's her secret?" I whispered.

"I don't care," Leon said. "Her secret doesn't interest me. Yours does."

"And what is that?"

"Well, you have a man who would walk to the ends of the earth for you. Who wants to care for you, be with you every minute of the day, be so close it's like we're one person."

"I know that feeling—the one person thing. I thought it would be too much for you, too close."

"Never."

"Tell me more."

"You're happy, and one day you'll have children, if that's what you want, and a house you'll always feel secure in. You'll never have to worry about anything—I'll be the one to do that—and if anyone ever hurts you, they'll have me to deal with. I'm your protector, your knight if you like, the man on the white horse who'll sweep you up with him and gallop you away to a castle that holds all our best memories."

"But what about our gang? They're going to want to be a part of our lives, a part of us. How do we explain we don't want that—or not much of it? I don't want to hurt their feelings."

"Everyone drifts away from their friends in the end, love. We all find other people to fulfill our needs. We can explain, but I don't think we'll have to. They're great people. They'll just know we need time alone."

"So how will we get that?"

"When we want to be by ourselves we'll pull up the drawbridge and cast spells so big thorn bushes grow, stopping people from knocking on the door. And when we want to be with others, we'll lower the bridge and I'll go out on my horse and chop the bushes down. That's your secret. It's there for you to take."

"I'll take it," I said, lifting my face and finally letting the tears flow. "Yes, I'll take it."

Chapter Eighteen

My flat was warm—I'd left the heating on low while we'd been away. Leon dumped our cases in the hallway, and I went straight to the kitchen, wanting a nice hot cup of tea. I laughed at myself. The vodka-loving woman in me had well and truly done a runner. Was this what happened when you fell in love? Did you change, mellow, become so unlike who you were before you didn't recognize yourself? I didn't care if it was. I liked me now, was comfortable with my feelings, my needs, and that was all that mattered.

Tea made, I carried the cups into the living room. Leon was sprawled out on the sofa in the darkness, the light from the TV flickering over him. Every so often the furniture on the left-hand wall lit up too, giving glimpses of my many books and DVDs. They didn't claim my attention for long, though.

I stood and stared at Leon, taking him in and the fact that he looked so comfortable there, like he belonged. His hair was tousled, as if one of the lads in the pub had ruffled it in jest after I'd made my shagging announcement. Stubble coated his jaw, and shadows beneath his eyes gave him a weary air. He must have been tired from the long journey home and I wondered why on earth we'd even bothered visiting The Rusty Nail. It could have waited until tomorrow night. Then again, as Leon had said when we'd traveled, I'd have bumped into Jen way before then, what with living next door to her. She'd have blurted it to the others before we'd had the chance and it was something we'd wanted to do ourselves.

"I can see you looking," he said, focus still on the TV. He held the remote loosely in one hand, pointed toward the telly as though he were getting ready to switch channels.

If I knew him like I thought I did, he wouldn't be actually seeing what was on screen. When I was with him he did nothing but tend to my needs. Maybe, in years to come, the TV would take all his spare time, but I'd reintroduce Pussy into our lives and prize him away from the dreaded black box.

I stepped forward and placed the cups on the table, coasters beneath, and smiled again at the change in me. Coasters. They'd rarely been used before and still held the shine as though they were brand new. The table was old, though, scarred from use during my misspent years, boasting signs of wear and tear from tea stain rings to wine and vodka splashes that had eventually eaten through the varnish where I hadn't wiped up the spills. A red wine splosh looked particularly revolting, like blood spilt from a nasty fight.

It reminded me of the safe house.

There had been times when me and Jen had drunk ourselves stupid in this room, laughed until we'd cried and our sides had hurt. We'd zonked out where we'd landed some evenings, waking in the morning to find our mouths felt like the bottom of bird cages, dry and in need of a fizzy drink to reawaken our taste buds, our bodies still tired from us having danced away the previous night. Those memories, they were real happenings yet they felt very *unreal*, as though I hadn't ever been that person and it had all been a dream.

"I like looking," I said, going to the sofa and patting his feet so he lifted them.

I sat and he propped his legs on my lap. I smiled at the domesticity of the moment, how we'd quickly gone from rampant, secret lovers to something more definite, established. Something more couple.

"I also like this," I said, stroking his leg.

"What, my shin?"

From the corner of my eye I caught him smiling. "No, this. The way we are."

"I knew what you meant."

"I know you did. Fucker." I held back laughter.

"Yep, I'm one of those. But only with you."

"I should bloody hope so." I paused, then, "You do realize that I'm still capable of turning into someone else, don't you?"

"I suspect you are. I saw how easily you became Pussy, Ponsonby and Yummypenny. Born to be an actress, you were."

"Hmm, but I mean someone miles away from those people." I smiled to myself.

"Like who?"

I waved my hand about casually. "Oh, you know, like a mad, deranged lunatic."

"Ah, we're back to the toothpaste and the hairs in the sink thing, are we?"

"Sort of. But I was thinking more along the lines of you only fucking me." I adopted a nonchalant air. "Because if you fucked someone else while we were together...well, I've always wanted to try out the role of Ball Chopper or Dick Slicer. Good name, that. Dick Slicer."

He shuddered and went to draw his legs up.

I laughed and slapped his thigh. "Makes you squeamish thinking about it, does it?"

"Just a bit. But I don't need to think about it or remind myself of what you just said. This is it for me. You're it for me. No Dick Slicer needed."

"That's nice to know."

"And it might also be nice for you to know that I'd become Dick Slicer myself if the situation were the other way round. Whoever fucked you, well, he wouldn't have a dick to fuck with after I got hold of him."

My smile grew wider. "I bet he wouldn't." I went for switching the subject. The idea of another man between my legs made me feel a bit peaky. "D'you want me to pass you your tea?"

"No, I want you to climb on top of me, press your beautiful, perky tits on my chest and snog me."

"Such a charmer..."

"I can be, if you want."

I thought about him as Mr Ponsonby. "Oh, I know you can."

I shifted his legs off me then stood and waited while he lowered them to the sofa. I climbed on top of him, pressing my so-called perky tits right where he wanted them and wedging one knee between him and the sofa back. My other leg had nothing to rest on so I dangled it over the side, my toes touching the floor.

"Um, this isn't going to work," I said, doing my best to stay on top of him. "If we try anything kinky, I'm going to fall off." My knee sank to the carpet. "And it looks like that's going to happen sooner than I thought."

"The floor's good," he said, stroking his hand up and down my back.

"It might be for you – if carpet burns are your thing. I don't care for them personally."

"What, not even on your arse? So you can feel them the next day?"

"No, definitely not." I mock shuddered.

"It would only feel sore like it did when I used the wooden spoon."

I cast my mind back. "Hmm, not so bad then."

"That was a good time, wasn't it?" He clutched one of my arse cheeks.

"It was."

"Something you'd want to repeat?"

"I might do."

"With me using something else? Something made for spanking?"

I widened my eyes and kissed the tip of his nose. "Someone's got a very saucy side."

"Someone makes me feel that way."

I kissed him then, lovely and slow, teasing his tongue. He held me tighter, pushing me down onto him. His hard cock dug into me, as did the remote control. I broke my mouth free.

"There's something between us," I said.

"There is. Not only is there the remote but something hard and throbbing."

"Indeed."

"What are you going to do about it?" He massaged my arse.

"I don't know. What do you *want* me to do about it?"

His cock twitched—he was making it do that on purpose, I was sure of it, letting me know he was impatient to get things started. The minx in me came out and I got up then undressed. He stared the whole time. The remote slid off his leg and onto the floor. He didn't bat an eyelid.

"I'm all naked with nowhere to go except here," I said, positioning myself at the other end of the sofa. I knelt, hands on the arm, and waggled my arse. "Oh. Would you look at the position I'm in? Anyone would think I was inviting a man to fuck me from behind."

"Yeah, that's an assumption I'd have made."

"That's what I thought. I mean, who would *do* this unless they wanted a nice hard cock slipped into their cunt?"

I smiled, waiting for him to move, to come up behind me and start this sexy business. He didn't. So he was going to make me work for it?

"And that nice hard cock," I said, slowly moving back and forth, would just slide right in, no trouble, because that cunt I mentioned? It's soaking wet."

He just about managed to stifle a groan.

"It's dripping for it," I said. And waited. "And the scent of it. You can tell it's so ready. That arousal is climbing toward its peak." I paused, knowing what I was about to say but wanting to shock him. "Tell me, can you smell *sex?*"

"I..." He cleared his throat. "I can."

"Mmm, me too." I rotated my arse, opened my legs as much as I could without falling off the sofa, and groaned. "Yes, I can smell it. And that cunt? It's aching. It needs that nice hard cock inside it. Stretching. Filling. Ramming in and out."

I was jostled as he moved, the sofa cushions dipping then rising as I imagined him changing position. He fumbled with something and the sound of a zip being dragged down had me smiling. He settled behind me then, between my legs, and pushed his erection against my arse crack—skin on skin. His zip bit into my flesh either side, a nice bite that got me going.

"You're a teasing little— Fuck it, Mandy."

"That's the idea," I said. "To fuck it."

"Who are you?" he asked, sitting the end of his cock at my entrance. "Who"—he eased in some more—"are you?" He thrust right in.

I gasped. That full feeling seemed fuller tonight. I worked my cunt muscles—on purpose, like he'd done with his cock—clamping him tight.

"I'm just me," I said.

And I was. Just me. A woman who'd learnt to be herself instead of having to pretend she had confidence or was sexually attractive. Leon had taught me that he loved me anyway, so me trying to be someone I wasn't was futile.

"I like Just Me," he said, starting up a slow rhythm of long strokes. "She's who I knew was in there all along."

"Tell me, what's her secret?" I gripped the sofa arm—he was working my cunt just right.

"She's got an amazing arse from what I can see. And the way her cunt is wrapped around my cock... She'd love seeing it, watching it slide in and out. But she's too busy clamping her muscles, too busy trying to get off."

I was. Chasing my orgasm was the name of the game. I wanted to see what it was like to be fucked as Just Me. So far it felt good. Intimate yet rude, what with the things we'd been saying to one another.

He sped up, holding my hips to keep me steady. A bubble of bliss built up in my clit, and I reached down to touch myself. I rubbed, firm circular strokes, and kept going as pleasure grew, that pre-orgasm excitement that told me any moment now I'd come.

"And when she makes herself come like that... I'm watching her. Leaning over to see what she's doing to that soaking little pussy. Fuck, that's hot. And shit, she makes my cock feel good. Christ, she's beautiful," he said.

I pushed back into him, wanting more fullness, and gritted my teeth. I was close, so damn close.

"And she's all *mine*." He shunted in — hard.

That did it. I strummed on, faster, and came, the force of it sweeping and violent. I moved backwards and forwards so his cock slid in the way I wanted it to — firm and forceful. He let out a series of indecipherable words and filled my cunt with hot cum.

"Mandy," he ground out. "I fucking love you, Mandy."

And I loved him. Wholly. Without reservations.

"Marry me?" he said, holding me tighter.

"Yes! God, yes!"

Forever, that's what we had now. Forever.

And ever. Amen.

About the Author

Geraldine O'Hara is a multi-published author in three pen names writing several genres. She lives with her husband, children, and three cats in an English village. She writes full time and is also a cover artist and blog designer. In another life she was an editor. Her other pen names are Natalie Dae and Sarah Masters.

Geraldine O'Hara loves to hear from readers. You can find her contact information, website details and author profile page at http://www.totallybound.com.

Totally Bound Publishing

Home of Erotic Romance